Death at Hallows End

LEO BRUCE

Death at Hallows End

ACADEMY CHICAGO PUBLISHERS

First US publication 2003 by
Academy Chicago Publishers
363 West Erie Street
Chicago, Illinois 60610

Published in England in 1965

© 1965 by Leo Bruce

Printed in Canada

Library of Congress Cataloging-in-Publication Data

Bruce, Leo, 1903-1980.
  Death at Hallows End / Leo Bruce.
    p. cm.
  ISBN 0-89733-516-3 (hardcover)
  1. Deene, Carolus (Fictitious character)--Fiction. 2. Inheritance and
succession--Fiction. 3. History teachers--Fiction. 4.
England--Fiction. I. Title.

PR6005.R673D38 2003
823'.912--dc21

                                    2003001846

CHAPTER ONE

"INTO THIN AIR," FINISHED Lionel Thripp, and leaned back as though he had effectively made his point.

It was not like this rather solemn solicitor to use such a melodramatic cliché, reflected Carolus Deene, but the circumstances were unusual.

"You've informed the police, of course."

"Oh, the police. Yes, I've informed them and they tell me they have the matter in hand. But that's not much comfort to Theodora, who is beginning to fear the worst."

Carolus, deep in a leather armchair in the solicitor's office, looked about him and thought it was an unlikely place in which to hear the rather startling story Thripp had just told. The firm was an old established one, so much so that the names of its two present partners, Duncan Humby and Lionel Thripp, were not among those in the firm's title, which was Merryweather, Priming and Catley. These, if they had ever been active in the firm's affairs, were lost in the Victorian past, and for thirty years no one but Humby and Thripp had sat behind the two mighty desks of the two inner offices.

Carolus had known both partners slightly for some years— they were in fact his own solicitors, though his call today, made at Thripp's request, had nothing to do with his own affairs. He had just heard that for three days Duncan Humby had been missing, and neither in his office nor in his household could anyone explain the fact. Some of the suggestions made by Thripp, in fact, came strangely from a staid solicitor and might have startled the inhabitants of the cathedral town of Newminster in which both he and Carolus lived and worked.

Carolus, however interested in facts given him, rarely made a written note but liked to get his details securely in his head.

"Just let us go over a few points again. You say Duncan Humby left here on Monday?"

"Yes. Immediately after lunch. He meant to return the same night."

"He told you the object of his journey?"

"Yes. James Grossiter had sent for him."

"He was going to Grossiter's home?"

"No. That was the first extraordinary thing. Old Grossiter was staying in this place—Hallows End."

It was extraordinary. Everyone in Newminster had heard of Grossiter, who was reputed, in mouth-watering local stories, to be a millionaire. He lived in a gloomy great house on a hill overlooking the town, and rarely left it. He was usually called Old Grossiter, though he was not in fact much older than the man referring to him, Carolus reflected. Sixty-five at the most, but something of a recluse if not a misanthrope, and certainly a valetudinarian.

"He was a client of yours?"

"Of Duncan's, more precisely. He did not recognise my existence in the firm, perhaps because I joined it three years later than Duncan."

"So he consulted Duncan?"

"I shouldn't say 'consulted'. To say he *instructed* Duncan might be better. As you know, he was an autocratic man and believed he knew a great deal about law. Duncan could handle him, I could not."

"Did you know he had left his home?"

"Not till Monday morning when Duncan came in and told me that Grossiter phoned on Sunday from Hallows End."

"What was he doing there?"

"That was the second extraordinary thing. He had gone to stay with his nephews who have some sort of a farm there."

"Any reason for his visit?"

"He gave none to Duncan. But some months ago his son Raymond, whom he had quarrelled with, died in Cape Town. Old Grossiter used to say he would never actually make a will to help his son, but that he didn't care if his son inherited as next of kin. One gathers that he couldn't kill all paternal feelings in himself, though he refused to have any contact or correspondence with his son. The original quarrel had been connected with a woman Old Grossiter had employed. But Raymond Grossiter had afterwards married someone else.

"When he and his wife were killed in a car crash, Old Grossiter seems to have realised that unless he did something about it, all his money would be inherited by his sister's two sons, Holroyd and Cyril Neast, who had this farm at Hallows End. He scarcely knew them and decided, so Duncan believes and I agree with him, to investigate the pair. He may also have had it in mind to see a man named Hickmansworth. This was the illegitimate son of his second sister and thus a cousin to the Neasts. They farmed neighbouring properties. Grossiter went to Hallows End, without telling anyone, some days before his death."

"How did the investigation go?

"One can only draw conclusions. On Sunday morning, at eleven-fifteen, he phoned Duncan at his home and told him immediately to draw up a will and bring it to him to sign on the following afternoon."

"Do you know what the terms were to be?"

"Yes. As far as anyone did. His whole fortune, which was considerable—though probably less than popular estimate has made it—was to go to charities, except for five thousand pounds to his charwoman, a Mrs. Cupper."

"Good gracious! *What* charities?"

"*Any* charities, he told Duncan. Cat and dog homes, orphanages, anything Duncan liked, so long as absolutely nothing could be claimed by his nephews. We had quite a morning, drawing it up and making bequests to our own favourite causes."

"I hope the animals were not forgotten?"

"They certainly were not. It was an interesting will. But there was one other point. When Grossiter gave Duncan these instructions on Sunday morning he added something which puzzled Duncan. He was to draw up an immediate Deed of Gift of ten thousand pounds to someone called Humphrey Spaull."

"Did the name mean anything to you?"

"Not to me. But Duncan has an excellent memory. Soon after he started to act for Grossiter, some twenty-two years ago, there was a similar gift of about half that sum to a woman called Edith Spaull who had been Grossiter's housekeeper. Duncan said it was to set her up in a profitable little sweet-and-tobacconist shop here in Newminster."

"I don't know it."

"No. Mrs. Spaull died some years ago and the shop was taken over with some others by the East Street Supermarket. This Humphrey Spaull, whom we knew nothing about, was apparently the woman's son."

"And did Duncan prepare this Deed of Gift?"

"He had not completed it when he set out on Monday. Grossiter emphasised that the will was the urgent thing. But Humphrey Spaull, whoever he is, would presumably have lost anyway, since it is almost too much to expect that the will was signed that afternoon before Duncan's disappearance."

"Why?" asked Carolus. "Stranger things have happened. Duncan might have left his car and walked up to the farm, seen Grossiter and been obliged to . . ."

"Oh, yes," said Thripp impatiently. "Everything's possible. But where is he now?"

Carolus was thoughtful.

"Meanwhile," he said at last, "have you any reason to know whether the nephews were aware of that telephone call? That is, did they know they were being excluded from inheritance?"

"It would seem not. Old Grossiter distinctly said there was no one in the house when he phoned. The two brothers had gone to church, he said."

"So it was with this will, all ready for signature, that Duncan left here on Monday."

"Just so."

"Did he go by car?"

"Of course. He drove his Jaguar. You know what Duncan was—is about cars. Motoring is still a hobby for him, though I must say I find it hard to understand. He and I are the same age, you know, and I've given up driving. But he still likes powerful motor-cars. He drives well, but I don't think he should speed as he does. That sort of thing could lead to a terrible accident."

"But it did not in this case?"

"No. His car was found intact by the side of a quiet road which led to the Neasts' farm, the church and nothing much else."

"You think he left it there?"

"It's hard to say. The keys of the car were left in it and the engine started at once when the police found it. There was no sign of any kind of struggle or anything of the sort."

"And no sign of Duncan either?"

"None. As I told you, he seems to have vanished into thin air."

"Yes. I noted the aptness of your quotation."

"As you no doubt are aware, Old Grossiter died in the small hours of Tuesday morning. Coronary thrombosis. He is being cremated tomorrow."

"Nothing questionable about his death?"

"Oh, nothing at all. The local doctor, an excellent fellow called Jayboard, has signed the certificate."

"Then Duncan's disappearance at that point was extremely convenient for Grossiter's nephews?"

"Of course. They inherit. That is what makes Duncan's disappearance sinister as well as mysterious. If he had reached Grossiter in time they wouldn't have inherited anything at all."

"Yet there is no reason to think they knew that Duncan was coming?"

"Unless in a fit of exasperation, the old man told them what he was going to do. He was a highly eccentric individual, as you know. Or unless by some remote chance someone remained hidden in the farmhouse on the Sunday morning and heard Grossiter phone."

"So, not to mince matters, Thripp, your inference is that one or both of these brothers may have been involved in kidnapping or even killing Duncan Humby before he could reach Grossiter?"

"I wouldn't say it was my inference," said Thripp cautiously, "but it does seem a possibility, doesn't it? What else can have happened to the poor chap?"

"I see what you mean, but there are several flaws in that, as even a provisional theory. Why did he stop his car at that point? Why did he get out of it without any sort of struggle?"

"He may not have stopped his car there. It may have been driven there after he had gotten out somewhere else."

"True. But the whole idea becomes unreal when you consider that Grossiter died quite naturally that night. It introduces coincidence, in which I have no faith at all. For if as you suggest the brothers prevented Duncan from reaching their uncle, Grossiter's death at that precise moment was too convenient altogether for them."

"And if his death wasn't natural?"

"The thing becomes clumsy and almost absurd. In order to prevent the making of a will which could prevent their inheriting, these two brothers dispose of the lawyer without leaving a trace of him and proceed to murder their uncle in a way which baffles a good doctor. All in one night. Does it sound convincing?"

"No. I must say that put like that it is incredible. But where *is* Duncan Humby?"

"That, presumably, is what you want me to find out?"

"Yes. I talked it over with Theodora Humby this morning. You know her?"

"Very slightly."

"She is, as you can imagine, in great distress. She agrees that you should be asked to investigate."

"Very well. Then I shall start at this end."

"At *this* end? What can you possibly want to know from us here?"

"First, what evidence is there that Duncan ever left Newminster?"

Thripp's eyes, usually rather expressionless, opened at that.

"Evidence? I don't know what you mean. Are you suggesting that he didn't drive to Hallows End?"

"I'm not suggesting anything. But do we know he did?"

"We know he had an appointment there. We know that when he left me he intended to keep it. And we know his car was found there. Isn't that enough?"

"Not really. As you yourself have said, anyone could have driven his car to that place. Anyone, that is, who knew he was going there."

"Extraordinary," said Thripp. "Such a thing had not occurred to me. I suppose, as far as we know, he may still be in
Newminster."

"He may be anywhere. Istanbul or Buenos Aires. Or under
the ground."

"I'm surprised to hear you talk in that sensational way. One
might think poor Duncan had deliberately disappeared."

"It is a possibility, on the facts so far as I know them."

"But what motive could he have?"

"There, my dear fellow, you raise a point of interest. Who
can possibly say what goes on in a man's mind? His wife? His
partner?"

"Ridiculous. There was nothing mysterious or introspec-
tive about Duncan. I'd worked with him for nearly thirty years.
He had a very open character."

"I should still feel happier if someone had seen him on his
way to Hallows End. Perhaps someone did. But I must point
out that we know absolutely nothing at present. Except that
he's missing."

Thripp looked earnestly at Carolus.

"You do realise the urgency of this thing?" he asked. "You
have, if I may say so, a reputation for discovering the truth
about the most extraordinary circumstances, but somewhat in
your own time, as it were. In this case there is poor Theodora
nearly out of her mind and I am in a state of extreme anxiety.
Quite apart from the personal side of it, there is the business to
think of. The disappearance of a solicitor naturally attracts a
great deal of attention. I have already received anxious enquiries from clients. If you are going to lose time in fruitless specu-
lations—well, I shouldn't say that—but in remote possibilities,
it will put me in an impossible situation."

"I see that," said Carolus, smiling. "But jumping to conclusions wouldn't help you, either. Do you know this place—Hallows End?"

"No. It's in a very lonely part of the country, I believe, a village with a thousand or two inhabitants. You'll go down there, of course?"

"Yes. After I've seen Theodora Humby. Now will you tell me one or two things about Duncan. He had, I assume, no money worries?"

Thripp looked impatient.

"Really, Carolus, you are only wasting time with questions like that. Duncan was—*is* a methodical and contented man. He had—*has* a substantial fortune . . ."

"Invested?"

"I never discussed that with him, but I should imagine in gilt-edged securities. Now . . ."

"He had no personal worries at all?"

"So far as I know—and as I've told you I am in a position to know—none at all."

"He had one son, I believe?"

"Yes. Alec. He's abroad."

"He and his wife were . . ."

"Theodora is a somewhat difficult woman, I imagine, but they had lived together for thirty years and I really don't see what their relationship has to do with the matter."

"Had Mrs. Humby money of her own?"

"Really, Carolus, this is absurd. I am asking you to find Duncan Humby, not to gather material for his biography."

"It may amount to the same thing. I would be glad if you would answer my questions so that I shan't have to come to you again."

"Theodora had no money of her own," said Thripp almost sulkily.

"You yourself had no disagreement with Duncan?"

"You don't have a long-standing business partnership without *some* disagreement. We got on remarkably well, on the whole."

"Had there been some recent disagreement?"

Thripp stood up and looked out of the window.

"Nothing that could have the smallest connection with Duncan's disappearance," he said.

"Do you mind telling me the subject of it, though?"

"I think it quite unnecessary that you should know and if I had supposed that you would waste time on such irrelevancies I should not have called you in. But I shall tell you now, to prevent any misapprehensions. I wanted to sell the practice and retire and Duncan was unwilling to do this. In a business like this it would be difficult and unprofitable to sell a partnership— it has to be all or nothing. Though Duncan and I are the same age, had been to school together as a matter of fact, he believed himself to be a more active man than I and didn't hesitate to say so. It had caused some—I won't say ill-feeling—some slight disaccord."

"Had the point about selling the business been decided yet?"

"Not actually. I had first suggested it six months or more ago and was growing a trifle impatient. But we remained on amicable terms and as a matter of fact lunched together on Monday before Duncan set out for Hallows End."

"Oh, you did. Where?"

"At the Crown. It's been our habit for many years to lunch together at the Crown once or twice a week. On this occasion we telephoned the manager, a man named Tuckly, to arrange for lunch to be served to us half an hour early because Duncan had, in front of him, the long drive to Hallows End and back. He was in high spirits at lunch and ate a good meal—more than

I should care to do. He has always been rather a big eater, but on Monday he excelled himself."

"So as far as we know, you and the waiters at the Crown are the last to have seen him?"

"He had to get his car from Mace's garage. I have confirmed with Mace that he did so at one-thirty. This would mean he would reach Hallows End, which is sixty miles away, somewhere about four, I imagine."

"And when was his car found?"

"Not until the following morning, I believe, but you will hear all that when you reach Hallows End. I hope that will be this afternoon?"

"Depends on whether or not Mrs. Humby can be seen before then. I don't want to start till I've had a talk with her."

"You don't seem inclined to think that Duncan's disappearance has anything to do with Grossiter's will and his two nephews at Hallows End."

"I don't say that at all. It may have everything to do with them. But if you mean do I expect to find Duncan, alive or dead, in a cellar of their farmhouse, I would say frankly, no."

Thripp nodded moodily.

"I hope you'll have news for me soon," he said.

"I'll tell you as soon as I have," Carolus promised, and left the somewhat overheated office.

CHAPTER TWO

COMING AWAY FROM THE solicitor's office, Carolus Deene had a premonition that this case would lead him into deep waters, perhaps into personal danger. This did not disturb him—on the contrary, he would be glad if the long series of problems he had successfully tackled would reach a climax with one that tried his mettle as a man of action as well as a theorist. There had been too much armchair detection recently, he thought, and although he had no ambition to be one of those heroic figures, forever in and out of hideous peril and armed to the teeth, those somewhat absurd men of action so popular in the modern world, he welcomed a case that would, he believed, give him wider scope than the mere whodunits of the past.

The first thing he had to decide about the disappearance of Duncan Humby was whether it had been voluntary or involuntary. If the first, he would take no part in the search. As he had said to Thripp, no one knows another man's mind, and if Duncan had chosen to disappear, he probably had excellent reasons for doing so which were no concern of anyone else. It certainly wasn't for him, Carolus, to take any part in restoring him to his wife and partner.

If, on the other hand, Humby was being held against his will, or if he had (and it was a possibility to be faced) been murdered, there was something unusually sinister about the crime. Humby was not a man to be easily forced into anything, and certainly not to be intimidated. He was in his sixties, but was tough and active and seemed ten years younger.

The story of Grossiter and his two nephews had an unpleasant ring to it, but, as Carolus had told Thripp, that was no reason for jumping to any easy conclusion, certainly not to such an obvious one as Thripp had suggested. But the thought of that deserted car with the ignition keys still in it on a lonely road near an isolated farmhouse, was to Carolus rather more than ominous.

He did not look forward to his first interview which would necessarily be with the wife of the missing man. He knew Theodora Humby, and considered her to be something of an hysteric, a woman who dramatised every situation so that a conversation with her was like taking part in an old melodrama. But there were certain things he had to ask her and he could, after all, discount the histrionics.

The Humbys lived in a large Victorian house on the outskirts of Newminster, a house that Theodora had renovated and spruced up with characteristic excess. The central rooms had been knocked into one with pillars to support the upper floor, and a wide staircase ran across the back of it.

The walls were white and decorated with gilt and coloured Spanish woodcarving and a suit of burnished armour stood in one corner.

The front door was opened by the housekeeper, a squat and realistic widow named Molly Caplan whom Carolus knew. She told him to sit down.

"Mrs. Humby will be with you in a minute," she said and gave a knowing look at the staircase by which, Carolus guessed, Theodora liked to make an entry.

He was right. She appeared at the top of the stairs in something that William Morris might have designed for his wife to wear if she was to be painted by Rossetti.

"Mr. Deene!" she cried. "Thank God!" She descended a few stairs. "I knew you would come!" From the foot of the stairs she extended both her hands and rushed towards Carolus. "Tell me at once," she said looking into his eyes, "is he still alive?"

"I expect so," said Carolus coolly. "I'm going to try to find out. Can I ask you a few questions?"

"Ask me anything. Anything! I have no secrets now. I have been in hell these last days. It is all a nightmare. I still cannot believe it."

"Believe what, Mrs. Humby?"

"That Duncan, of all people, would vanish in this extraordinary way. He was, you know, the most conventional of men."

"You think, then, that he may have disappeared deliberately?"

"Impossible! He was utterly incapable of such a thing. He would never deceive me in that way. Never! He told me everything."

Carolus wondered where he had heard those deluded words before. From sad experience he knew that when one of a married couple used them of the other, they nearly always indicated their exact opposite.

"Did he for instance tell you why he was going to Hallows End that afternoon?"

"That," said Theodora emphatically, "was a matter of business. He never discussed his clients and I never asked him about the details of his work. Such inquisitiveness would be quite foreign to me. I meant that between us there were no *personal* secrets. If he had even thought of going away for a time I should have been the first to hear."

"Did he discuss his finances with you, Mrs. Humby?"

"Certainly not. I should have considered that vulgar."

"Really? Between husband and wife? It would seem to me very natural."

"Perhaps I am rather exceptional in that, Mr. Deene. I take no interest in money. There was always sufficient for me to have the few simple things I wanted, and that was all I asked. Only once did the subject arise between us."

"That was?"

"A trivial matter. I came on a notebook of his from which I gathered that he had some money in a Swiss bank. I made no remark, I need scarcely say, but he seemed to think it was incumbent upon him to give explanations. He took great trouble to do so,"

"And what were his explanations?"

"I scarcely recall the details now. Such things were beyond my scope. But . . . it was something about holidays abroad and a Labour government. He thought he might be prevented from taking sufficient money for our annual jaunt."

"Did you happen to notice what sort of sum he had abroad?"

Carolus thought he caught a quick keen look on her large-featured face.

"There was no indication of the amount," she said. "And of course I never asked him. But this surely is beside the point. Where is he now? That's the question."

Ignoring this, Carolus asked about Duncan's passport.

"Then you *do* think he has run away?" cried Theodora, raising her hand to her cheek.

"I'm really only asking the most obvious questions," said Carolus. "Clearing away some of the undergrowth. Thripp has asked me to try to find your husband and I can only do so with your help."

"Of course. I see that I mustn't draw foolish inferences. His passport, *entirely* by coincidence, is with him. That afternoon he wore an old overcoat that he hadn't put on since we returned from Denmark. His passport was in the pocket."

"How can you be sure of that?"

"My good Caplan noticed it some weeks ago. She never interferes with anything and left it there. Besides, it is nowhere to be found."

"You have looked? Then you too must have had some idea that your husband might have gone abroad?"

Theodora looked a little confused.

"I had nothing of the sort," she said at last. "I was merely doing what you said you were doing—clearing away the deadwood. I *know* that Duncan would not go even to London without telling me."

"Did he mention that he was going to see Mr. Grossiter?"

"Grossiter? Who is he?"

"A client of your husband's who had summoned him urgently to Hallows End. It was in order to sign a new will which your husband had drawn up."

"So that was why he went! He certainly said nothing about that to me. As I told you, he never discussed business. Did he see this Grossiter?"

"Apparently not. But his car was found near the house where Grossiter was staying. As perhaps you know."

"I know nothing except that my husband is missing. If it weren't so tragic it would be almost squalid. Like those photographs one sees in the paper."

"I knew your husband a little, Mrs. Humby. I gathered that he took great pride in his physical fitness."

Theodora rose to her feet dramatically.

"It was a fetish!" she said. "I told him so many times. Because he was *not* fit, really. A dickie heart, ever since he had rheumatic fever. Dr. Boyce told him so a score of times. 'Don't overdo it,' he used to say. But Duncan was so courageous. He would never give in to that sort of advice. He drove his car, played eighteen holes of golf and a fast game of tennis. He even *danced*, Mr. Deene. Not with me, I may say. He was a powerful man. 'Brawny' would be a better word."

"He could take care of himself in any trouble that might arise, you think?"

"I only saw him fight once. That was in the south of France one year. I was angry at the time because it made us so conspicuous, but he did it for me, in a way. A man was most insulting. Duncan knocked him down. But like *that*, Mr. Deene. We walked away and left him on the ground,"

"How long ago was that?"

"Not long. Duncan must have been in his fifties at the time. You may discount any thought of his having been kidnapped if you had any idea like that. Duncan would never allow it."

"You must have something to account for his disappearance, though," pleaded Carolus.

"I never theorise," announced Theodora. "But I must confess to you that I begin to have the blackest forebodings. I *know* that he is not absent by his own wish. I *know* that he would never give me a moment's anxiety if he could help it. Then what remains? I ask you, Mr. Deene. What possibility remains?"

"Several," said Carolus. "Loss of memory. An accident. Sudden illness."

Theodora shook her head. "No! No! I have intuitions, Mr. Deene. I can see only one way of accounting for his disappearance and it is the most terrible. But how or why it can have happened is beyond my imagination. It is for you to discover that."

"I hope it may not be. I hope we shall find some other explanation. I am going tomorrow to Hallows End and when I have even the smallest information I'll phone you or Thripp at once to tell you what I can."

He had a most uncomfortable feeling about Theodora Humby. It was as though her habit of dramatisation demanded to be fed with more startling events, as though she would in some macabre way almost enjoy receiving news of her husband's death. This did not mean that she was indifferent to him. She might even love him in her fashion. But she was clearly a pathological case and her histrionics were a kind of outlet for her emotions.

She was very quiet now. Carolus thought there was something furtive, almost snakelike in her eyes as she looked aside at him.

"You think you will find him?" she asked.

"How can I say?"

"Exactly. How can you? We know nothing really. Do we even know that he left Newminster?"

"His car . . ."

"But many people can drive a car. Anyone who knew that he intended to go to Hallows End might have driven it there."

"But who did know?" asked Carolus. He could scarcely believe that her suggestion pointed in the direction it might seem to point.

"That is for you to discover, surely. I certainly did not. But someone must have done."

Carolus kept his eyes on her face as he asked the next question.

"Surely he told you that he would be later than usual in coming home that evening?"

"He did! Of course he did! But it was quite casually that he mentioned it. A matter of business. He had to drive out somewhere to see a client. He would get something to eat on the way back. Nothing more was said."

"On the way back. Then you gathered that he had to go some considerable distance?"

"I gave very little thought to it at the time."

"Is it possible that he said anything to Mrs. Caplan?"

"Ask her, Mr. Deene. Leave no stone unturned! If my good Caplan knows anything she will tell you at once. I will take you to her little sitting room. She will be watching the television now. Unless there is anything more you wish to ask me?"

Carolus was silent for a moment. He felt certain that Theodora knew things that would be valuable, but he doubted whether she herself was aware of this. He decided that until he had gone farther and could make his questions definite and explicit, it was useless to press her with vague enquiries.

"No. Nothing," he said. "At least for the present. Yes, I should like to see Mrs. Caplan."

"You shall. Come with me. She is so much more realistic than I am. I can only wish that I were as unimaginative as she. Imagination, in circumstances like these, is a terrible thing."

They found Molly Caplan warming her toes before a bright coal fire. When she saw Carolus she switched off the television.

"Mr. Deene would like to ask you one or two things," said Theodora. "I shall leave you together. You know him, don't you? If anyone can help us it is he!"

She left them in a dramatic and purposeful way, shutting the door firmly behind her.

Molly Caplan smiled.

"You're not fooled, are you?" she said. "Theodora's terribly upset, really. You mustn't think because she behaves like Ophelia that she's not suffering. I know she is."

"I'm sure she must be. Yet I can't help feeling that in some way she enjoys that suffering."

"Could be," said Molly Caplan sharply. "What do you want to know from me?"

"To be frank, I can't really say. Anything you like to tell me, I suppose."

"Do I think he's left her, for example. No, I don't. It was a strange relationship, but they were fond of each other. He was a bore with all his health and fitness and she as you know is a tragedy queen, but somehow it worked. He would have said he made allowances for her, but really she did for him. A man in his sixties who did physical jerks before a window every morning and threatened to take up yoga can't have been easy to live with. I've been in the house five years and I'd describe them, without hesitation, as a happily married couple."

"You think he confided in her?"

"There was nothing much to confide. He never talked about his business, if that's what you mean."

"Never? Did *you* know for instance that Thripp wanted to sell their practice and Duncan Humby wouldn't hear of it?"

"As a matter of fact I did. Lionel Thripp is an old friend of mine. It was through him I came to look after Theodora and Duncan. But I think it's perfectly possible that Theodora didn't know that. Duncan made a point of not talking shop."

"So she would not have any idea where he was going that day?"

"None, I should say. Not an inkling."

"Had you?"

"What?"

"An inkling?"

For the first time Molly Caplan looked a little uncomfortable.

"I don't see why you should ask. How can it possibly help your enquiries?"

"It may not. But someone must have known, apart from Thripp."

"Yes. I knew. But not from Duncan Humby. I think we won't go into that any farther."

"All right. Just tell me how long you had known?"

"Well, since the previous evening. Now . . ."

"What's your theory, Mrs. Caplan?"

"Don't have one. But it looks pretty ugly to me. Duncan's an obstinate man. Someone might have to kill him before he'd give in."

"Unless he could be fooled or persuaded into something incautious,"

"Most unlikely,"

"You have a car, Mrs. Caplan?"

She stared at him.

"What on *earth* . . ."

"Nothing, really," said Carolus, smiling. "It's a question I may have to ask several people in Newminster. Call it a formality."

"I have a car, yes," said Molly Caplan sulkily.

"Did you use it that Monday?"

"This is absurd, you know. Mondays are my days off. Naturally I used my car."

"But you don't feel like telling me where you went?"

"I certainly don't. I find your questions impertinent and foolish."

"They must seem so. I'm sorry. Will you at least tell me at what time you took your car out?"

"Immediately after lunch, of course."

"And you returned?"

"Before midnight. Now that's enough."

"Your car is a . . ."

"Ford Consul. Blue," snapped Molly Caplan and stood up as though to dismiss him.

Carolus left the house after going back to say goodbye to Theodora. He had a pretty shrewd idea of the two women, if nothing else.

He decided to go over to Hallows End next day, and was irritated to find thick fog. Last Monday, the day on which Duncan Humby had left his partner in order to go to Hallows End, had been a clear September afternoon, he remembered, and later as he walked home from a friend's house, Carolus had noted a bright sky with the stars unhidden by clouds. Wherever Humby had been that evening, his movement had not been concealed by the weather, unless it was very different at Hallows End.

He reached his comfortable little house to find Mrs. Stick, his housekeeper, in some agitation.

"Wherever have you been, sir?" she asked. "I've phoned everywhere likely and couldn't get word of you anywhere. The Headmaster's been ringing up every half hour or so. He sounds as if he's in a state."

Carolus, whose position as Senior History Master at the Queen's School, Newminster, had never yet prevented him from undertaking an investigation, nodded calmly.

"If he phones again, tell him I've come in."

"There it goes now," said Mrs. Stick, a small resolute-looking woman with steel-rimmed glasses and a thin mouth. "That's him, for certain." She hurried to the receiver. "Yes, sir. He's just come in. No, I'm sure he'd be pleased. Five minutes? All right. I'll tell him." She turned to Carolus. "He's coming round at once," she said as though she was announcing Nemesis herself.

CHAPTER THREE

CAROLUS DEENE WAS AN odd kind of schoolmaster and it was his conscience, or something very like it, which kept him to the grindstone. A commando officer during the war, he had lost his young wife in an air raid and had returned to what at first seemed a lonely and meaningless existence. He had inherited a large private income, but he did not attempt to live on it idly. He decided to teach, thus filling his empty days with timetables and textbooks, tiresome pupils and breaks in the common room, a routine which he varied only when a chance came to exploit his flair for the investigation of crime.

He had discovered this flair in himself by writing a book called *Who Killed William Rufus? And Other Mysteries of History,* in which he applied the methods of modern criminal investigation to certain historical events with lucid and sometimes startling results. From this academic diversion he had been drawn to look into a local murder which a friendly CID officer was investigating, and from there he had never looked back. Slight, taut, rather good-looking and elegantly turned out, he was a well-known figure in Newminster. As a schoolmaster he was more popular with the boys than with other members of the staff who were inclined to resent his wealth and the Bentley Continental he drove.

The Headmaster, a large portly man named Hugh Gorringer, appreciated Carolus's ability as a teacher but was frequently alarmed by his involvement in sordid crime that he feared would bring Carolus's name unpleasantly into newspapers and "smirch," as he put it, "the good name of the Queen's School." Mr. Gorringer's own redundant and cliché-ridden speech had become familiar to Carolus who found it, if anything, rather endearing. He treasured many of Mr. Gorringer's more resounding pomposities.

This evening Mr. Gorringer was breathless as he entered Carolus's sitting-room, and his large hairy ears were crimson with cold or dyspepsia, Carolus frequently wondered which. His protuberant eyes were wide.

"Ah, Deene," he said. "I am relieved to find you have returned. Alarming news, my dear fellow, alarming news. Duncan Humby has not been seen for four days."

"Three," said Carolus.

"You know, then? It is more than distressing. He was not only the father of one of our Old Boys, but had recently joined the Board of Governors. Any scandal that touches him touches the school."

"Do sit down, Headmaster. What will you drink?"

"You know I seldom indulge, Deene. But in the circumstances—perhaps a little Scotch whisky with some soda water would not come amiss."

As though forewarned, Mrs. Stick appeared at this moment with a tray.

"Scandal?" said Carolus thoughtfully. "It's not scandal I'm afraid of. It's murder."

There was a sharp slam of the door as Mrs. Stick left them. She disapproved even more than Mr. Gorringer of Carolus's involvement in what she called "all these horrible murder cases."

Mr. Gorringer goggled.

"Murder?"

"It begins to look rather like it. Did you think he was just running away from his wife?"

"I did not know what to think. My apprehensions have all been for the school I have the honour to . . . command, to direct. This point of view does not seem to have occurred to you, Deene," he added reproachfully.

"Quite honestly, it does seem rather secondary. I have been to see the man's wife this afternoon."

Mr. Gorringer screwed his face into an expression of incredulity.

"Am I to gather, then, that you have already become in some way associated with these circumstances?"

"Thripp asked me to look into them," said Carolus casually. "I don't know whether I shall, unless I think there has been a murder. If Duncan Humby has simply made a bolt for it, it does not interest me."

"Deene, I find that an immoral—I was almost going to say a cowardly, attitude to take. I have sought you out today for some mite of comfort in this distressing affair. You seem determined to turn it into one of your murder cases, to make it even worse than the disappearance of a School Governor."

"Really, Headmaster, that is unreasonable. I don't seek for murder. It comes about too often for that. Humby may be found alive and well at any moment, which will settle the whole matter."

"But will it?" asked Mr. Gorringer tragically, "You may not be aware of all the circumstances. There is a woman living in his house called Caplan."

"Yes. I know her."

"It has come to my ears . . ."

"No. No. You're not going to suggest that there was anything between Humby and Molly Caplan?"

"Fortunately it is not as bad as that. The red tongue of slander has not gone so far as to suggest that a School Governor would so disgrace himself as to indulge in an intrigue in his own house, under his wife's eyes, with a housekeeper."

"Then what does the red tongue of slander suggest, Headmaster?"

"I fear it is no idle suggestion. There is too much concrete evidence to support it. The woman Caplan was surreptitiously meeting the other partner, Thripp."

"Well, why not? He's a widower, she's a widow. For all you know they may mean to get married."

"It's a bit too much of a coincidence, Deene. This secret liaison, then the disappearance of the employer of one party and the partner of the other. Doesn't that speak volumes?"

"Frankly, to me it says nothing at all. Even if Humby has been murdered . . ."

"Deene, I should prefer that you avoid reference to that most remote and unpleasant possibility."

"It has to be faced. I couldn't make the blindest guess yet, though. I'm going down to Hallows End tomorrow."

"To Hallows End?"

"Where Humby's car was found. He had an appointment there, you know, which it seems he never kept."

"You seem wholly committed, Deene. Must I remind you that we begin the new term in eight days' time?"

"Should be cleared up by then," said Carolus cheerfully. "One way or the other."

"Or the other," echoed Mr. Gorringer in a graveyard voice. "You are incorrigible, Deene. There is something positively ghoulish in your attitude. I can only plead with you, as I have so often done in the past, to see that no unpleasant publicity shall attach itself to you and to protect the good name of the school. Moreover I would remind you that we have our usual staff gathering, on the day before term begins, to settle some points in the syllabus. Hollingbourne has indicated that he has several interesting matters that he wishes to add to the agenda. So that all extraneous interests of yours, my dear Deene, will, I sincerely hope, be completely disposed of before then. We would like the benefit of your closest personal interest in our academic affairs. *Il faut cultiver notre jardin*, as Voltaire said."

Mr. Gorringer rose.

"I will leave you now to your meditations. I shall hope to hear what progress you make. This case, as you know, touches me dearly."

Alone, Carolus took another drink. Going over the scraps of information and hearsay he had gathered made him restless and dissatisfied. He knew nothing yet. A lawyer had disappeared and this had released the usual small scandals, things which might not have come to light otherwise. But whether they were of the slightest relevance or interest he had no idea. His thoughts were interrupted by the entrance of Mrs. Stick.

"Your dinner will be ready in just five minutes, sir," she said sharply. "And I'll thank you to come straight through when I tell you because there's a suffle."

"A what, Mrs. Stick?" asked Carolus, honestly puzzled.

"A suffle. That's what it calls it in my book. You've had it often enough."

"A soufflé!"

"That's what I said. And there's a nice bit of somon poshee to follow."

"Splendid, Mrs. Stick."

Carolus saw that she was hesitating and had something on her mind.

"I heard what you said to Mr. Gorringer, sir. Well, I couldn't help it. So it's murders again, is it?"

"Only one, if that," said Carolus.

"You'll excuse me, sir, if I ask whether it has anything to do with this lawyer who's disappeared? Because Stick happens to know something about that."

"Stick does?"

"It's not that he'd want to get Mixed Up, or anything. Only knowing what he does he thought it was only right I should Speak. I'm sure I don't know what my sister would say if she knew I was passing information over anything of this sort. It would send her right off, I shouldn't be surprised. But right's right. Stick wouldn't sleep if he thought he was holding anything back."

"What on earth does he think he knows?"

"It's not a matter of think. When Stick says anything, which isn't often, he's sure of what he says. What it turns out is this lawyer was going to see old Mr. Grossiter that day he was never heard of again."

"I know that. But how does Stick?"

"Never mind that for now," said Mrs. Stick, becoming animated. "Mr. Grossiter had gone to stay with his nephews and it had made him want to make his will against them. Not that he's to be blamed for that. It seems from what's been said that these two nephews of his was nasty sort of customers when it came to it. Living all alone out there! Small wonder the old gentleman wanted to make sure they shouldn't get nothing."

"How *do* you come to know all this, Mrs. Stick?"

"It's not me. It's Stick. I wouldn't demean myself by having anything to do with it from the first. But you know what Stick is."

"I'm beginning to think I don't."

"Well, he's got a conscience, that's one thing. He met a lady at the Chequers where he goes sometimes, to the saloon bar for a glass of light ale. When my sister came down from Camberwell she and her husband went with him so I know it's all right. This lady, a Mrs. Cupper, a very respectable party, told him about this man Darkin."

"What man Darkin?" asked Carolus desperately. He had never known Mrs. Stick so garrulous.

"This one I'm telling you about that works for Mr. Grossiter. Mrs. Cupper works there too, you see. She knows Darkin well of course and run into him again yesterday. He'd come over to get his black things for the funeral which is to be tomorrow. Or rather cremation."

"Mrs. Stick, do you think I could ask Stick himself about this?"

"No, sir. It wouldn't be a bit of good. He wouldn't like to say anything. But I can tell you what there is to know when you've had your dinner. I don't want that suffle spoilt."

Three-quarters of an hour later Mrs. Stick resumed.

"He's Chapel," she said.

"Who is?"

"This Darkin. That's why we've never seen him at St. Luke's. It seems he's one of the smarmy types. All right to your face."

"You say be worked for Grossiter?"

"Been with him for years, so Mrs. Cupper told Stick. He must have gone with him to this place where his nephews live because he talked all about it to Mrs. Cupper yesterday. He's not a man who says much in the ordinary way but he seemed to want to tell Mrs. Cupper about it. His boss had Gone very sudden, it seems. Very sudden, he told Mrs. Cupper. He wasn't with him when he Went, but it was him who found him dead. He wouldn't say any more than that, but putting two and two together, he must have been very attached to the old gentleman. Well, he'd been looking after him for years. The old gentleman wouldn't go anywhere without he took this Darkin with him. And when he died like that no wonder Darkin was upset."

"What was his job with Grossiter exactly? Valet?"

"You could call it that, I suppose. He did everything, as far as I can make out. Looked after his clothes and medicines and that. The old gentleman didn't like a lot round him and at the house here in Newminster there was only this Darkin and Mrs. Cupper who went in for cleaning. But Darkin thinks something of himself. Mr. Grossiter's companion, he says he was, and likes to be called Mister Darkin."

"You say the cremation's tomorrow?"

"Yes. At eleven o'clock she told Stick. Over at Beaslake where there's one of these crematorium places. There won't be many there, Darkin said, because the old gentleman was never one for a lot of friends. But his two nephews will be there and Darkin and a few more, I daresay. Only what I don't understand, if I may be allowed to say so, sir, is whatever made you start talking to the Headmaster about murder. There was nothing funny about the way poor old Mr. Grossiter died, if that's what you're thinking."

"No, no, Mrs. Stick," Carolus said. "But as you yourself said, a lawyer from Newminster has disappeared rather mysteriously, and when there is a disappearance like that there is always a chance of murder being the explanation."

"There is if *you* have anything to do with it. You may be sure of that. So it's all to do with this place Hallows End, then? I suppose that means you'll be going over there, getting mixed up with I don't know what?"

"But you've just been giving me valuable information, Mrs. Stick."

"Ah, that was Only Right. Stick had to speak and neither of us won't have anything to do with the police, as you know well enough. But it doesn't mean we want to see you start all over again, missing meals, coming in at all hours and us never knowing from one minute to the other who's coming to the door. It's time you stopped these larks, sir, it is really. Flesh and blood won't stand it. Why, in that last case the judge reprimanded you and all the papers were full of it."

"It was the coroner," said Carolus mildly.

"Whatever it was, it wasn't Nice. People Talking and that."

"Let's hope they have no cause to this time," said Carolus and walked firmly across to the telephone. When he picked up the receiver, Mrs. Stick left the room.

He dialled the number of an intimate friend of his, a local doctor who looked after the school and had a busy practice in the town. His name was Lance Thomas, but he was known as Dr. Tom. He and his wife Phoebe had befriended Carolus when he had first come to Newminster.

"Hullo, Lance. How are you both? Good. Tell me, was old Grossiter a patient of yours?"

"Yes. Why?"

"I'm rather interested. He died very suddenly, didn't he?"

"So I understand. It wasn't totally unexpected in his condi-tion."

"No?"

"Well, no. The local man is an old friend of mine. We were at St. Thomas's together, as a matter of fact. Splendid chap and a first-rate doctor. I'd begged him not to bury himself down in that end-of-the-world village but he did it for his wife who came from those parts."

"He saw Grossiter?"

"Yes, and signed the death certificate."

"You're satisfied with his examination?"

"Oh, absolutely. I'll give you the technical details if you like, but it's the sort of thing no doctor could make a mistake about. Certainly not Stanley Jayboard who has tended to specialise in it."

"What sort of thing? What exactly did he die of?"

"Call it a heart attack. That's near enough for a layman."
Lance Thomas chuckled. "A perfectly natural death. No doubt
about that."

"Do you think anything could have happened to cause such
an attack? Would the patient have to be given a sudden alarm,
or piece of bad news, or anything of that sort?"

"Really, Carolus! All this investigation is going to your head.
You're beginning to be melodramatic. No. Nothing of that sort
would be necessary. There *could* have been something, perhaps,
but there's no reason whatever to think so. Stanley doesn't, anyway. Why? What are you up to?"

"I'm interested. Duncan Humby was on his way to see Grossiter. His car was found half a mile from the house. As you
know, he's disappeared."

"It's curious, isn't it? Could be coincidence."

"But it never is. For me coincidences simply don't exist."

"You had better go and see Stanley Jayboard. Tell him you're
a friend of mine. He may be able to help you."

"Thanks, Lance. Grossiter is being cremated tomorrow."

"Yes, I know. Stanley's quite happy about that. Though I
gather he's not fond of the nephews."

"You're not going to the cremation?"

"Lord, no. I'm worked off my feet just now. That was why
I was so grateful to Stanley for signing that certificate. I ought
really to have gone as the old man's regular consultant. But
don't say anything about that, Carolus."

"Of course not."

"Ask Stanley if he remembers that night at Vine Street.
Hooliganism, the magistrate called it next morning."

"I will. Did you know Duncan Humby?"

"Just. He wasn't a patient of mine."

"All right, Lance. Thanks for the information."

Carolus dropped into his favourite armchair and remained perfectly motionless for some twenty minutes. Then he fell asleep.

CHAPTER FOUR

CAROLUS DECIDED NEXT DAY to drive down to Beaslake for Grossiter's cremation. He was curious to see who would attend and interested in getting a glimpse of the two nephews Holroyd and Cyril Neast, and perhaps of the man Darkin whom Mrs. Stick had heard described as "smarmy." He also reflected that he had never yet attended a cremation and felt a certain morbid curiosity about it.

He hurried over his breakfast and as he opened the front door called back to a scowling Mrs. Stick that he would not be in to lunch, He was soon out on the main road driving fast to Beaslake.

The crematorium was an ugly red brick building with vague suggestions of ecclesiasticism about it. The ground near it was taken up with a large car park, and there were many shrubs of the least interesting varieties. Here, if anywhere, Carolus thought, there should be cypresses, the funeral trees that the Romans dedicated to Pluto because once they are cut they never grow again. Yews would take too long to grow, perhaps, for one could not imagine this public library sort of building becoming an ancient monument that would one day inspire some twenty-fifth-century Gray to compose an "Elegy written in a Country Crematorium."

Leaving his car in the car park, he walked across to the entrance where a cheerful man in black was picking his teeth.

"Morning," the man said. "You for the Grossiter lot? It's not till eleven, so you've got nearly an hour to wait."

"I know," said Carolus. "How long will it take?"

"Well, they've ordered the big show, organ, parson, *the lot,* so it will be half an hour at least. We do a shorter one cheaper, but these Mr. Neasts wanted no expense spared."

Two men, the first arrivals, entered by a side door.

"Are they attending the cremation?" asked Carolus.

"No. Two of the cooks," said his bright interlocutor. "They've got a big day on today. We've got half a dozen in all, but two of them's being done together. Yes, an 'usband and wife. Killed in a motor smash. So that'll take half the time. We shall have to get your lot out pretty smart though because we've got another at twelve and the Reverend Gillow hates being late for his lunch. I've known him cut out a piece of the service if it's getting past half past twelve, though not the part about dust to dust and ashes to ashes because they always notice that. Yes, I will have a cigarette. You'd think I was a non-smoker working here, wouldn't you? But I like a pipe. My wife pulls my leg about it. 'I don't know how you can', she says, 'when you've been at that place all day.' You get used to it, though."

"What happens to the ashes?" asked Carolus.

The man understood that he did not mean those of his pipe.

"They can have them if they want them. We're very strict about that. Some don't bother, though. They reckon that once anyone's gone they're gone and a lot of ashes won't make any difference, any more than what you rake out of the stove in the morning. Others are just the opposite. They buy special pots for them and keep them on the mantelpiece. I shouldn't care for that myself, would you? Not to think your old man or whoever it was in the room all the time sealed up in an urn. But the best are those that want to scatter 'em somewhere and go to a lot of trouble to do it. That's generally in the will. Sometimes they hire a boat and take 'em out to sea or climb up some hill or other when there's a high wind. Seems a bit silly to me but there you are. If it's left in the will they've got to do it, haven't they?"

"What arrangements have been made for the ashes this morning?"

"They've got to be kept. The nephew was most particular about that. Hullo. This looks like the first of them. I must go and slip my gown on. Oh, yes, I always do that. Looks more serious, doesn't it? It doesn't do to be cheerful round here. Would you like to go inside? You can sit down then."

"Yes," said Carolus. "Somewhere at the back if you don't mind."

"Come on, then. This way. You can sit here where you won't be noticed, if you like. Oh, thank you, sir. You can see all right from here? That's where they put the coffin when they bring it in."

Carolus looked about him. He was in a church-like building with a chancel in which was a curious structure for the coffin. Beyond it was something in the shape of an altar with a brass cross and two candlesticks. Seeing him looking at this, the man beside him explained.

"They can have the cross or not, just as they like. A lot on the free-thinking side don't care for it, but there's others that do. Same with the parson. You don't *have* to have him. A good many of them like to read out bits of poetry or something of the sort for themselves. It's all according. But Grossiter's lots C of E. They're having hymns and that. The organ's at the back and there's a choir of four—three ladies and a man. Mr. Pye's the organist and I always think he's a bit loud. I'd like a bit more hush about it. Well, I must run along now. The hearse'll be here any minute."

It was a quarter of an hour, however, before the coffin was carried in, followed by the two brothers Neast, and some way behind them came a tall dark man with huge hands and feet whom Carolus took to be Darkin. All three of them looked unctuously solemn. There was no one else.

As well as he could, Carolus examined the brothers Neast. He had watched their faces only in profile as they passed, .and now could see no more than the backs of their heads. Both had thick dark hair growing far down their necks, both had long narrow heads and rather prominent ears. But otherwise there seemed little resemblance. One, who was tall and narrow-shouldered, was pale and somewhat saturnine. The other, much shorter, looked powerful and heavy and had a red bad-tempered face. They wore, Carolus guessed for the first time, stiff uncomfortable suits of black with starched collars and black ties.

The organ finished playing the Dead March and a form of funeral service was read by a sleek little parson in a surplice. Its climax came when the coffin which, it now appeared, was on an electrically-operated lift, began to disappear slowly into regions below, and the words of the parson took a consolatory and resurrectionary turn. It was all rather unpleasant.

Carolus waited until the brothers and Darkin had left the building, then came out in time to see them getting into a Rolls Royce driven by Darkin—the property of the late Mr. Grossiter, Carolus suspected.

Carolus found his recent friend standing beside him.

"I don't know how you feel," the man said. "But if you were thinking of a drink, there'd just be time for me to come down with you to Feathers and get back before the next lot. If we was to go in that car of yours."

Carolus nodded and they walked towards the car park.

"Reverend Gillow brings a thermos when we've got two on in one morning, and Mr. Pye's a teetotaler. But I must say I find a drop helps you through it, though I don't always get a chance."

They pulled up at the Feathers and found themselves alone in a small bar divided from the saloon by a partition.

"Was you a friend of the departed, sir? Or of those brothers Neast?"

"Neither, really. I wanted to see a cremation."

The man laughed.

"Well, you've seen one," he said. "Funny turn-out, isn't it? I shouldn't like it, not for myself I wouldn't. I told the wife, I want to be buried when my time comes. I can't understand people asking to be frizzled up like that. Can you?"

"There may be reasons sometimes," Carolus said.

"You mean if there's anything funny about the way they've gone? There's always that. I believe if the police could stop it altogether, they would. Look at the evidence that may get destroyed."

Carolus said nothing and the man began to talk about the ceremony just completed.

"They haven't paid for it yet," he confided.

"We understand they're going to come into all the old gentleman's money and it's a big lot, but they haven't got much in the meantime. Seems funny with them being farmers, doesn't it? They've got a name for being close, though, so perhaps they don't like paying for it out of their own money, as it were, and are waiting to get his. You never know with people, do you?"

Carolus agreed that you didn't, and at his friend's request ran him quickly back to the crematorium for what he had described as the next lot. Then Carolus drove across country towards Hallows End which lay some forty miles from there.

It was a raw ugly morning with rain threatening and a misty chill lying over the flat uninteresting countryside. The journey was tedious because he was cutting across the direction of the main roads by narrow by-roads, sometimes no more than lanes, and they kept his speed uncomfortably low.

While still some four miles from the village, he had to follow a main road for a few hundred yards, and on it saw a bright new pub called the Falstaff Hotel. Its neo-Elizabethan architecture and expanse of diamond-paned windows did not attract him, but since it was likely to be the only place for lunch in the vicinity, he decided to follow the instruction on a large board: "Drive In." Another board proclaimed: "Lunch now Being Served in the Tudor Dining Hall," and yet another: "Accommodation for Motorists." When, however, he reached the Sir Walter Raleigh Bar, he found that these inviting inscriptions, at least for today, had been unproductive for he was alone with the landlord, a youngish man with a large and turbulent growth of hair on his upper lip.

"Good-o," said the landlord, "you're the first today. You must have a drink on me. What'll you have?"

Carolus accepted his usual Scotch and soda and prepared to face the other's evident curiosity.

"See you've got a Bentley," said the landlord. "Envy you. They're fab. Absolutely fab."

"They're good," said Carolus.

"Good? They've marve. Wish I could afford one. Nothing better, car-wise."

Carolus deftly turned his line of thought.

"Do you know the village of Hallows End?" he asked.

"Know it? Born there. Father the rector before the present man. You going there? Press, perhaps?"

"No," said Carolus.

"But I'm interested in recent events round here."

"Mean this joker who's disappeared? Incred, isn't it?"

"No. Nothing's incredible. How do local people account for it?"

"They don't. They can't. Unless it's a murder. They've no experience of that sort of thing. Murder-wise we've had nothing in the village this century."

"Has there been any attempt to connect it with Monk's Farm and Grossiter's death?"

"Shouldn't think so. Why should there be?"

Carolus believed in giving a little information sometimes — a sprat to catch a mackerel.

"The man who disappeared was on his way there," he said. "He'd been called by Grossiter to make a new will for him."

"Oh! Was that it? I see what you mean. Well, the Neasts are pretty unpop round here but I don't think anyone connects them with this empty car. They've lived here a long time. Stranger-wise the folks are a bit suspish, but not of one of themselves. See what I mean?"

Only just, thought Carolus, but nodded encouragingly and ordered two more drinks,

"Not sold on mysteries myself but it's oddish now you come to mention it. This Grossiter had only been at the farm a few days and no one would have known he was there if it hadn't been for a character called Darkin who worked for him. He came here every night and told us. I thought him a bit obnox myself, but I listened to him. Scandal-wise we don't hear much in these parts."

"What did he tell you?"

"A lot, really, up to the old man's death. Then he never said another word. In fact he hasn't been in since. Seems Grossiter was rich and had never made a will. His only son died recently, so unless he did something about it these Neasts would get the lot. The old man had never seen them till he came over here to find out what he thought of them."

"And what did he think?"

"Not much, we gathered. Now you tell me about this solicitor it all falls into place. Pretty ug, isn't it?"

"Not necessarily. Humby may turn up. His disappearance may be nothing to do with the Neasts or Grossiter."

"Extraw, though. Coincidence-wise that would be absolutely incred to me."

"Do you know the Neasts?"

"By sight, of course. Haven't seen them to speak to since I was a boy. Old man sent me to Repton, then I was at the university for a couple of years."

"Ox or Camb?" asked Carolus, infected by the landlord's habit of abbreviation.

"London, as a matter of fact. Then I bought this place about three years ago. But the Neasts never come here. In fact they're very little seen about. Invis, you might say. Never enter a pub. Do their own housework. Go to market over at Cashford every Monday. Otherwise keep to themselves."

"They must employ someone on their farm."

"They had two men. But that's another death we've had. Old Harold Rudd died a few days before Grossiter. He was buried on the Saturday."

"Oh, and what did *he* die of?"

"Overwork, I should think. He was in the hospital two miles from here. Swanwick Hospital. He was about seventy. So death-wise we've been pretty biz."

"I didn't know anything about that. The Neasts have another man?"

"Yes. Joel Stonegate. Has a cottage just down the road here. Looked after by his daughter."

"Does he come here?"

"Not often at lunchtime. But he's in the public bar most evenings. The police went to see him the day before yesterday."

"What for?"

"Because he's the only one who saw that chap in the car, so far as anyone knows. It appears that Stonegate felt ill that afternoon and left his work about four o'clock. As he was cycling down the Church Lane that leads from Monk's Farm to the village he saw this car by the side of the road. He says the man in it was asleep. You can ask him about it tonight, if you like. He'll talk about it for hours if you let him. He's told the police and the press, so I'm sure he'll tell you. We don't get much happening round here sensation-wise."

"You said just now the Neasts go to market at Cashford on Mondays. That's an unusual day for a market, isn't it?"

"Tradish," said the landlord. "Cashford Market's been held on Monday for centuries, I believe. Yes, they usually go."

"Do you know if they went that Monday?"

"I seem to remember Joel Stonegate saying so, but I can't be cert. I'm not too hot, memory-wise. But you can ask him yourself this evening."

"Thanks. I will."

"Take it you're CID?" said the landlord.

Carolus reflected that this was the first time anyone had made that mistake.

"No," he said. "But I've been asked by his partner to try to find Duncan Humby, the man who has disappeared. That's what has brought me here."

"Sort of private investigator?"

"Something like that. What can you do about some lunch?"

"Well, we're pretty slack at this time of year. I'm afraid there's not a fire in the Tudor Dining Hall. But food-wise we're all right if you like to have it here by the fire. Fact the wife said she had something pretty delish for today."

"That's fine. As soon as it can be managed then."

The landlord disappeared and presently his wife, a rather sullen young woman, appeared, to lay a cloth on one of the glass-topped tables. She did not seem to enjoy her work.

"There's only sheep's hearts," she said.

"Thank you," Carolus smiled. "I like them very much."

"It's a good thing you do because that's all we've got. It's no good laying a lot in at this time of year."

"Of course not. Very kind of you."

"You can have some soup first if you want it," she melted sufficiently to say.

"Excellent."

"And there's a treacle-roll for afterwards." She was brightening rapidly. "But I don't expect you care for that."

"I love it," said Carolus truthfully and wondered what Mrs. Stick would say.

"Like some sprouts with your heart?"

"Thank you."

"There's a nice Stilton, too."

"It's a banquet," Carolus told her.

"I knew there'd be suffish," put in the landlord. "Catering-wise the wife's terrif, really. Only she doesn't shout about it."

"No, and I don't call a twelve-by-twelve little dining-room the Tudor Hall and then have to ask people to eat in the Saloon. And I don't put up a notice saying lunch being served now, when there's not a soul in the house," she retorted, her irritation returning with a rush.

As she went out, the landlord grinned at Carolus.

"That's the way they are," he said. "But I don't expect I have to tell you that. Woman-wise I bet you're pretty expier."

CHAPTER FIVE

IT WAS A COLD AND gloomy afternoon of low clouds and a threat of rain when Carolus left the Falstaff Hotel and took the road to Hallows End. He wanted to have a look round the village and the road to Monk's Farm before meeting any of the people with whom he intended eventually to become acquainted.

The road was not wide and its many curves were not made easier to take by the high hedges which ran on each side of it. But he passed nothing except a small farm lorry, which obligingly pulled hard in and waved him past. Even so, it took some twelve minutes to cover the four miles.

The village, when he reached it, appeared to be a rather dreary collection of small houses with one or two larger ones hiding behind dense shrubs. It had an overgrown and neglected look and its streets were almost empty of pedestrians. There was a pub, the Ploughman, and a few shops, including a post office, general store, a butcher's and a family grocer's, all of which would have benefited from a coat of paint. No church was visible and if the Rectory was here, it was indistinguishable from other larger houses.

However, he decided not to spend time on enquiries at the moment but to take the road out to Monk's Farm, the road beside which Duncan Humby's car had been found. He had to ask the way to this and stopped beside a gnomish little man hobbling along with a twisted stick, a de la Mare creature with sharp eyes under thick brows.

"Monk's Farm?" the gnome said. "What you going there for?" Amused, Carolus told him he had business.

"Oh," said the gnome and stared at him without giving any information.

"Could you . . ."

"You going to see those Neasts?"

"Yes," said Carolus, without impatience.

"Queer lot," said the little man and stared again.

"The same road leads to the church, doesn't it?"

"Church is beyond the farm. I don't know whether you'll find those Neasts about up there. Police have been to see them."

"I can try," said Carolus, "if you'll tell me . . ."

"They've just lost one of their men. Old Harold Rudd. Lived in a cottage near the churchyard. Died over at Swanwick in the Ospittle. His old woman's still in the cottage."

"Really? Which way do I go?"

"Those Neasts have just come into a lot of money from their uncle."

"Yes. I know. Is this the road to their farm?"

"He was Took too. Funny, isn't it? Just after old Harold Rudd. Then there's this fellow disappeared."

"Quite. If I drive . . ."

"They don't know where he is and I don't suppose they ever will."

"You don't? Perhaps you know where his car was found?"

"I know all right. Just opposite where there's three elms standing together on the road to the farm."

"But which *is* the road to the farm?"

"That's where they found his car. But they can't find him. How could he have got away from there without anyone seeing him? That's what I want to know."

Carolus resigned himself.

"Is it a big farm?" he asked.

"Not extra. They pulled the old house down years ago. Otherwise it would have fallen down. Rotten all through, they said. Neasts built themselves a bungalow when they came here."

There was a pause and Carolus made a last desperate attempt.

"You said the road . . ."

"I didn't say nothing about it. But no more did you say what you wanted up there. Still, I'll tell you. Keep on down here for a bit and you'll see it turn off to the right. It's got a notice up Church Lane. Take that and you'll come to it. Not more'n a mile away. You pass my cottage on the way. The only house you do pass. I've lived up Church Lane for years."

"Thanks," said Carolus and drove on.

He found the turning. The road here was truly narrow but after a few hundred yards broadened slightly. He looked out for the three elms standing together and, when he was approaching them, stopped.

Yes, it was possible for a car to be in to the side here and for another car to pass it. But only just. If Duncan Humby was still at the wheel of his car when it stopped here, he must have deliberately pulled it in to leave room for others. There was no sign of any wheel tracks on the grass edges, but that meant nothing, for it had rained since. If there had been anything of the sort, presumably the police would have seen it when they were first informed. He was accustomed to coming too late into an investigation for that sort of evidence and knew that it was not, in any case, his strong point.

He drove on. When he first saw the house at Monk's Farm, he thought that if the old character in the village had not told him that it was a bungalow he would never have recognised it as a farmhouse at all. It was large as bungalows

go, but shoddy-looking and bare, with no attempt at a garden about it. It had the ugliness of a blatantly new building
set in otherwise unspoiled surroundings. It was some distance from the farm buildings which were farther down the
road, so that it was necessary, presumably, for the brothers
to come out of their silly little front gate and walk a few
hundred yards on the tarmac road every time they wished to
reach the fine old buildings of the farm, which were unspoiled
by corrugated iron.

Carolus took this in as he passed slowly on his way to the
church that he could see ahead. It was a surprisingly fine Norman
building, and, like so many churches in the eastern counties, far
too large for its present parish. As he approached it, he saw
ahead of him a small clerical figure on a bicycle. They reached
the church's gate at the same moment and smiled at each other.

"Come to see the church?" said the Rector, a rotund and
cheerful little man in his forties.

"It looks very fine from the road," said Carolus noncom-
mittally.

"It *is* very fine," said the Rector, who always spoke with
such emphasis that he seemed to think he was giving his hearers
a surprise with each new sentence. "I could sometimes wish it
was not so fine and large, but a mile nearer thc village. I might
be able to fill it then. As it is we're lucky if we get a dozen to
Mass on Sunday. But we get scores of people on weekdays coming to look at the architecture."

"You're High Church then?" said Carolus who had no idea
the Rector would not care for the expression.

"We're Catholic," said the Rector smiling. "'High Church'
is a dated term used by Protestants and such. Like to have a
look around?"

They entered the church together.

"We're particularly proud of the font," said the Rector, waving his hand towards it. He went on to speak informatively of ecclesiastical architecture, particularly as exhibited here.

When Carolus could venture to turn the conversation, he asked if the brothers Neast were among the Rector's congregation.

"Unhappily we don't see eye to eye on a number of points. They go over to Swanwick where my colleague Sumper provides them with eleven o'clock service and all that sort of thing. I understand they are very devout in their own way, but they heartily disapprove of what they call my popish practices. The east window . . ."

Carolus had lost him again.

"I believe you buried one of your parishioners last Saturday," said Carolus when there was a momentary pause.

"Yes. Poor old Rudd. A dear old sinner who never came near us though he lived a few yards away. His wife is a little better. She does sometimes turn up for Evensong. I came out this afternoon to have a look at the grave, as a matter of fact. Mrs. Rudd wants to erect quite a mausoleum over it, I gather."

Carolus accompanied him towards the proposed site of this.

"Are you serious about a mausoleum?" he asked innocently.

"No. But it's rather a large affair of the old-fashioned slab kind which will look a bit out of place among more modest gravestones. See what you think."

They went into the churchyard and saw a fresh grave still earth-covered.

"If I had guessed what she wanted I'd have had Rudd buried elsewhere. I hate ostentation. But farm workers are highly paid nowadays and they can afford this sort of thing. I never expected it of Annie Rudd, though."

They reached the lych-gate.

"My Rectory is in the village. I know my wife would be delighted to give you a cup of tea if you would care to call. I'm going straight back there."

"That's awfully kind of you, padre. I'm afraid I can't make it today, though. I have to see the Neasts."

"Ah," said the Rector inscrutably.

"Why is theirs called Monk's Farm?" Carolus asked.

"Because it was the monks' farm," said the Rector with enthusiasm. "This was the church of a fair-sized abbey which was destroyed in Henry VIII's reign. The farmland stretched over the very ground the Neasts occupy now. There was a beautiful old house, I believe, but the Neasts pulled it down when they came. Or so I've been told. It was before my time."

"They have something pretty hideous in its place."

"It's not beautiful, is it? But I daresay more convenient. Well, I must leave you, I fear."

They bade each other goodbye and the Rector was soon cycling vigorously homeward.

Carolus had no intention of calling on the Neasts at this point, but when the Rector was well out of sight, set out on foot for a cottage beyond the churchyard, which he presumed was Rudd's.

A knock brought a tall and powerful-looking elderly woman to the door where she stood arms akimbo.

"Mrs. Rudd?" he enquired.

"Yes." She sounded dubious and peered at Carolus in the failing light.

"I'm a friend of the man who disappeared from his car down the lane here. I am trying to find out what has become of him," Carolus explained.

"But whatever has that got to do with me, may I ask?" She was not hostile, but seemed genuinely puzzled.

"Nothing, I'm sure, but I thought I had better see everyone living up this lane."

"You better come in to the fire, then. We can't stand shivering out here in this cutting wind."

Carolus followed her into a lamplit kitchen where a coal fire burnt in the range. She told him to sit down and did so herself.

"I don't know why you should ask me," she said. "I was too taken up with my husband's dying to know anything about it."

"Your husband worked for Neasts?"

"Yes, for fifteen years. It was only when the new laws came in that they paid him properly, but then they couldn't help it. He was all right in the last few years but his working stopped him from drawing his pension."

"He died in hospital?"

"Yes. Cancer. He'd been feeling off for some time and I kept telling him, why don't you go to the doctor, I said. When at last he did go it was too late. He had a lot of pain towards the end. I don't like to think about it, really."

"Which day did he die?"

"On the Wednesday and buried on Saturday afternoon. There was a lot turned out for it and I must say the wreaths was lovely. Reverend Whiskins, well, Father Whiskins he calls himself, did the burial service. They'd brought the body over from the hospital at Swanwick, you see."

"I understand you are putting a very fine memorial over his grave."

"Well, I like something with a bit of show to it and Mr. Neast has been very good about that, I must say. I thought to myself they could underpay him all those years, then want to make a lot of it when he's gone. Still, I must say they've been very good about it."

"They lost a relative of their own two days after your husband was buried," Carolus remarked.

"Yes. I heard about that."

"You never saw the gentleman?"

"No. According to what I hear he only came to the farm a few days before he died, and never went out so far as anyone saw. They only had the doctor to him after he was gone, so they tell me. It seems funny, doesn't it?"

Carolus thought that if he heard the word "funny" misused again he would throw up the case. It was beginning to haunt him.

"Do you remember last Monday afternoon, Mrs. Rudd? That was the day on which my friend set out for Hallows End and disappeared."

"Not specially, I don't. It was a nice afternoon, if that's what you mean."

"Did you go out?"

"Not to say out, I didn't. I fed my chickens and shut them up about five o'clock, I should say, then I was busy looking at the cards from the funeral."

"When you were out of doors, did you hear anything unusual?"

"Goodness me, whatever do you mean?"

"From the farm or anywhere?"

"I shouldn't have heard anything from the farm. not if they were all murdering one another. It's too far away. Besides, there was no one there. Mr. Stonegate went home early that day because he wasn't well, and the Neasts was over at the market at Cashford."

"You don't know what time they came back?"

"Well, they're usually back by about five, but of course I can't say to the minute. I didn't see or hear anything of them that evening but then I wouldn't, would I?"

"And since then? Have you noticed anything unusual?"

"Not to say unusual I haven't. But there's one man I don't like the look of, that's the one they call Darkin who came with the Neasts' uncle. Him I don't like the look of at all."

"I wonder why?"

"Well, why doesn't he go away now the old man's body's been taken away and cremated? What's he still hanging round for, that's what I'd like to know. I saw him this afternoon creeping round all in black and I said to myself you're a nice one, aren't you?"

"The cremation was only this morning, Mrs. Rudd."

"But what's he coming back here for? His job's finished, isn't it?

"Have you spoken to him?"

"I had to answer civil when he spoke to me, saying he's sorry about my husband and that. If you ask my opinion he's not all there, the way he looks at you. There's something funny about him anyway. Why, what's the matter, sir?"

"Nothing. Nothing. You were saying?"

"Yes, well, I don't like him, that's all. I never did from the first. He's Chapel, too. I heard him on about the Reverend Whiskins one day. What business is that of his, I'd like to know. If Reverend Whiskins is a bit on the High side and likes a few candles and that, it's us who've got to put up with it, not him. I saw him yesterday morning prowling round the church and the churchyard as though he'd like to blow it up. And when he went down to my husband's grave, I went out to him. 'You keep away from that,' I said. 'That's no business of yours.' 'I was only admiring the flowers,' he told me. 'Well, you admire them somewhere else,' I said. 'That's my old man's grave, that is, and it's not for other people to come nosing at.' He went off after that but I was glad I told him."

"You don't feel so strongly about your late husband's employers?"

"No. I can't say I do. They're a funny pair, there's no mistake about that, but not like what this Darkin was. Mean? Well, they *are* mean. I've never known them do a thing for anybody. But they've lived here a long time and we're used to them, as you might say. They've never said a word out of place to me, anyhow."

"What about the other man on the farm, Joel Stonegate?

"Stonegate? Oh, he's all right, I suppose. My husband and he never really got on, but I don't say the fault was all on one side. I've nothing to say against him. And he sent a lovely bunch of chrysanths to the funeral besides coming with his daughter."

"Thank you, Mrs. Rudd. You've been most helpful."

"I can't see how anything I've told you will help to find the gentleman missing, I'm sure. Was he coming to the farm, do you know?"

"He was on his way to see Mr. Grossiter, the Neasts' uncle."

"That accounts for it, then."

"For what?"

"For his car being up this lane. No one hardly ever comes up the lane unless it's to see the church, and there's a nice few in the summer do that. You see it doesn't lead anywhere after here. As soon as I heard about the car being there in the evening I said to myself, whatever was it doing in this lane, then? But what you say accounts for it."

Carolus rose to bid her goodbye and as he did so was surprised to hear someone descending the narrow staircase of the cottage. He had assumed that Mrs. Rudd was alone, and looked enquiringly at her.

"That's my lodger," she said, but offered no further explanation.

Carolus heard the front door open and someone go out into the night, but it was too dark to see.

"I didn't know you took lodgers," he said.

"No more I don't usually. But when Rudd was taken to hospital and I was on my own here, it seemed a chance, and he's a very quiet young man."

"Has he been here long?"

"He came the day after Mr. Grossiter arrived at the farm, I think it was. The Rector sent him to me. He's studying for an exam and sits reading books all day and writing bits on little sheets of paper. Doesn't go out much."

"You say he's a young man?"

"Not more than twenty-two or three I shouldn't say he was. He's very polite and that, but it wouldn't do for anyone to offend him, either."

"What makes you say that?"

"He practises boxing and that. He's got one of these punch balls up in his room and thinks nothing of lifting weights up and down which would do for anyone else. There's only one thing I don't like about him—that's his young lady. She came over to see him last Monday. I could see at once what she was."

"What was she?"

"No better than what she ought to be, and with airs and graces of I don't know what. Spoke to me like dirt, she did. She was trying to get him to do something he didn't want to, too. 'You *must* do it,' I heard her say. No, I didn't like her."

"What is your lodger's name, Mrs. Rudd?" asked Carolus.

"Spaull. Funny name, isn't it? Humphrey Spaull."

Carolus bade Mrs. Rudd goodbye and went to his car to drive down to the village. He was determined to make one more call tonight, but to leave the Neasts until tomorrow. First, however, he would have to phone Mrs. Stick, and for this he drove to a phone box which he remembered seeing in the centre of the village.

His housekeeper answered in alarmed tones.

"Yes? Who is it? Who? Oh it's you, sir. It gave me quite a turn ringing here with the house empty."

"Isn't Stick there with you?"

"Stick? Oh, yes. He's here. Your dinner will be ready in an hour. I've got a nice lapper oh for you."

"*What* did you say, Mrs. Stick?"

"You're having rabbit tonight."

"Oh, I see, yes. *Lapereau.* But I'm afraid I shan't be back, Mrs. Stick. I'm still sixty miles away. I think it would he better If I stayed the night here,"

"Well, of course it's not for me to say but you never know what damp sheets you may lie in and catch your death. I don't say anything about the dinner, though I did marinade the rabbit yesterday and was going to cook it ar lar Bordelice with a bottle of Bow Jolly. Still, if you want to eat some rubbish they give you *out,* you must do as you think fit. Oh, and there's a policeman called. A Sergeant Snow. He said he'll be in Newminster tomorrow again and will call on you about seven."

"What did you tell him, Mrs. Stick?"

"You know very well what I told him. Not if I had my way he wouldn't call, I said. But it's no good talking. I'll put the rabbit back in the marinade and tell Stick to double-bar everywhere. We can't tell who may be hanging round in the night, now you've got mixed up again. Good night, sir."

CHAPTER SIX

CAROLUS HOPED FOR GREAT results from the call he meant to make in Hallows End that evening, and in any case realised that for a particular reason it was necessary before he tackled the Neasts. Joel Stonegate, cycling home that Monday afternoon at about four o'clock, according to the landlord of the Falstaff, had actually seen Duncan Humby in his car. With any luck he might remember the car's position in the road, so that Carolus would know whether or not the Neasts could have passed it without difficulty on their way home from market.

But before he went to Stonegate's cottage he decided to have a drink at the Falstaff and book a room for the night. From the licence plate above the door he learned that the landlord's name was John Sporter.

"Found your friend yet?" Mr. Sporter greeted him. "No? It's pretty diff, I suppose. I know I shouldn't be much good detective-wise."

"Have you a room for tonight?" asked Carolus.

"Natch we've got a room. That's what we're here for."

"Good, Then keep it for me, will you? I'll be back in about an hour, I expect. And if you can manage something to eat I'd be grateful."

"I don't know what the wife can do dinner-wise but there'll be something."

"I want to call on Stonegate. I think you said his cottage was near here."

"About halfway to Hallows End. You can't miss it. It's the only thatched cottage on that road. But if you wait till about eight o'clock he's almost sure to be up here. He's pretty reg."

"I think I'd like to see him on his own ground," said Carolus and went out to his car.

The cottage door was opened by a meaty young woman who did not immediately speak.

"Could I see Mr. Stonegate?" Carolus asked.

"Dad!" called the girl in a weary voice. "Here's another one."

There was an incomprehensible call from behind her.

"He says come in," the young woman told Carolus. "He's just finished his tea."

Joel Stonegate was a heavy man in his late forties who wore glasses, at least to read the evening paper that was spread out before him. He did not get up to greet Carolus, but said with a little condescension, "Well, which is it this time? Press or police?"

"Neither," said Carolus.

"Neither, eh? That's something new. We've had the lot here, haven't we, Doll? Anybody would think I'd got this chap who disappeared locked up in one of the bedrooms."

"I wish you had," said Carolus. "It would be a great relief to a number of people. I'm trying to get some news of him, you see. Both his partner and his wife have asked me to do what I can."

"And being as I was the last to see him alive you come to me? That's just as it should be." He leaned back in his chair complacently.

"But were you?" asked Carolus.

"Was I what?"

"The last to see him alive."

"What do you think they've all been coming to see me for? The London papers sending down special reporters for an interview? Photographers flashing at me morning, noon and night? The police queueing up for interviews? If I wasn't the last to see him alive, I'd like to know who was."

"So would I," said Carolus. "But I didn't mean that. I meant *was* he alive? When you saw him?"

"I don't know what you're getting at. He was fast asleep."

"How do you know?"

"How do I know? Because I saw him. That's how I know. It's not the first time I've seen someone fallen asleep over the steering wheel of a car."

"But Mr. Stonegate, did you get off and open the door of his car?"

"Certainly I didn't, and wouldn't do such a thing, either. I should call it presuming."

"I mean, is it not possible that he was already dead when you saw him?"

"I don't know why you should get hold of such an idea. He looked as peaceful as a baby. I did just get off my bike and take a look through the window of the car and I could swear he was asleep. Had a few drinks at lunchtime, perhaps. The idea of him being dead never so much as came into my mind."

"Exactly. But now that I mention it, can you be sure, looking back? Did you notice any movement, for instance?"

"No. He was well away. I'm the same myself, once I'm off to sleep wild elephants wouldn't wake me."

"No, but a couple of reporters would. You'd be up quick enough if someone had come to interview you," put in Doll sourly.

Carolus decided that it was not much good pursuing this point. Stonegate had thought at the time that Humby was asleep and now nothing could make him doubt it. Whether he was, or whether he was dead might be established later but not from Stonegate's evidence.

"Can you give me any idea of the time when you saw him?"

Stonegate sighed.

"They all ask me that," he said. "And the police kept on about it. Most important, they said it was. I can only work it out from what time I got home. That was twenty past four by that clock over your head now, and I rode straight home here. Say it was a little before four when I saw him and you won't be far out."

"Thank you," said Carolus. "That *is* important. But there's something which to my mind is more important still."

"Oh," said Stonegate haughtily, "and what might that be?"

"Just where on the road the car was standing."

"By those three elms."

"I don't mean that. Would you try to recall whether it had stopped on the crown of the road or pulled into the side."

"I don't need to *try* to recall. I can see it as plain as a pike-staff. It was near enough in the middle."

"Then had another car come along it couldn't have got past without moving it?"

"I wouldn't go so far as to say that."

"But the road is narrow there."

"It is that. No, I don't suppose a car could pass without going over the grass border. Now you come to mention it, I'm sure it couldn't."

"Yet your employers, the two brothers Neast, must have been able to do so unless they moved the car to one side."

"I see what you mean."

"They were out in their lorry that day?"

"Of course they were. They'd gone to the market."

"And they weren't back when you left the farm?"

"Certainly they weren't or I should have told them I was going . . . It's funny, isn't it? I mean that's where the car was found in the morning."

"No, it was found on the side of the road."

"You think the Neasts pushed it there?"

"I don't think anything so definite. But somebody must have, since you remember it so clearly as being in the middle."

"Could have been the chap himself. Woke up and saw where he was and drew into the side before he dropped off again."

"I suppose it could, if he was merely sleeping when you saw him."

"I don't know why you keep on about that. The chap was asleep."

"Then you may be right. He could have driven it to one side himself. Was the car still there when you went to work next morning?"

"I see you know very little about it," said Stonegate loftily. "It was me who reported it to the police."

"When?"

"Next morning when I got to the farm. As I was riding there on the Tuesday at my usual time, which is before eight because I leave here at seven-thirty, I saw that car in the same place."

"In exactly the same place?"

"Well, I thought so at the time, but now I know it was nearer into the side."

"And the man was no longer there?"

"Not a sign of him. The first thought I had was that the car must have broken down so he must have walked on to the farm and the Neasts would know about it. So I went on to work, where Holroyd Neast was out in the farmyard. He's the older one, you know."

"The taller of the two?"

"That's him. I told him about seeing this chap asleep in the car on the afternoon before, but he didn't seem much interested. I said the car must have been there when he and his brother came home from market and he said yes, he had noticed a car in the road but hadn't thought much of it. I told him the chap was no longer there and he said no of course he wasn't. Who was going to spend a night in a car at this time of year when there were pubs and places handy? He could have got a room at the Ploughman in Hallows End or taken the taxi from the village somewhere else. So I told him I thought we ought to inform the police, I said, because it looked a valuable car and couldn't stop there forever."

"What did he say to that?"

"'Stonegate,' he said, 'you will be sorry to hear my poor uncle died during the night and I'm too upset to bother about a car left in the road.' I said I was sorry to hear about his uncle, though as a matter of fact I'd never seen the old gentleman, who stopped at home for the most part. Then Holroyd said, 'If you think you should, ring up the police straight away. Yes, that would be best. You go along to the house and phone.' So that's what I did and if I hadn't of done, it might have been another day before the police knew there was something funny going on. Did you say anything?"

"No. No. Please continue."

"The inspector at Cashford congratulated me on what he called my prompt action and sent Gallup the constable at Hallows End to see what it was all about. I don't think much of Gallup, he's too fond of pushing his nose in where it's not his business, but I told him what I knew all the same. 'You've done very well, Stonegate,' he said, 'and I must go and telephone to headquarters and report the whole matter.' So that's how I came to be recognised as the last man to see this chap alive and the first to inform the police. That's what the papers have been on at me for."

There was another unexpected interruption from his daughter.

"Oh, show him your picture in the *Swanwick Reporter* and have done with it," she said. She was evidently tiring of the whole thing and the self-importance it had given her father.

"Let' s see. Which one's that? Ah, yes, I know the one you mean."

"There's only been the one," said Doll to Carolus. "He's been watching all the other papers but it never come out."

"Tell me, Mr. Stonegate," began Carolus, heading off a possible quarrel, "did you gather from the questions the police asked you that they suspected you of knowing more than you said?"

"Whatever do you mean?" asked Stonegate.

"That's what *I* said," put in Doll with some animation. "The way they kept on you'd have thought they suspected Dad of doing away with the man himself!"

"Now you keep out of this, my girl," said Stonegate. "And talk of something you know about." He turned to Carolus. "I don't know what you're getting at, but the police was never anything but complimentary with me. As they ought to be."

"I didn't mean that. I am sure they were very polite. But did they ask you any questions about your own movements? Did they ask what you did on the Monday evening after you'd seen the man in the car?"

"Well, just to complete their records they had to, didn't they? Of course I took no offence and told them straight out. I'd come home from work feeling ill and I went to bed straight off, didn't I, Doll?"

"How am I to know what you did? You know very well I was staying with Frede over at Swanwick that night."

"I went straight to bed," said Stonegate loudly, "and stayed there. There was nothing to get up for and I had a nasty chill."

"You was better next day when I got home," said Doll sulkily. "Well enough to eat the best part of a steak and kidney pudding, anyway. Then telling them all about your being the last to see the man alive. You hear what this gentleman says? You may not have been. He may have been dead as mutton when you saw him. And if he wasn't he may be alive now, for all you know. Where would you be then with your 'last to see him alive'? I hope he does turn out to be."

"So do I," said Carolus heartily. "There are just a few more things I'd like to ask you, Mr. Stonegate. You've been very patient. Now when you reached the car that Monday afternoon, did you notice any wheel marks in the grass?"

"He'd never have noticed if there had been," said Doll. "He never notices anything except what's on the plate in front of him."

"As I see it," Carolus hurried on, "if any car had come up the road behind the Jaguar at the time when you found it, that car would be forced onto the grass border to pass."

"There was nothing of the sort," said Stonegate. "Otherwise . . ." he looked fiercely at his daughter. "Otherwise I'd of noticed it for certain."

"And when you found the car again in the morning?"

"Neither there was then. I couldn't help but see it if there had been."

"Was there anywhere about there for a car to turn?"

Stonegate thought deeply.

"Not for a hundred yards or more away from there, there wasn't. But some way back towards the village there's an entrance to a field belongs to Mr. Harker, a big farmer whose ground joins on to the Neasts' and the Hickmansworths'. He keeps his place up better than what they do and he's had some stones put down between the road and the gate. If anyone wanted to turn a car there he'd have to back in to that to do it. But it might not show because the tractor goes through there."

"You saw no one else in the road up to the farm that afternoon?"

"Didn't I, then, and told the police so. There was a chap going the same direction as I was. I passed him just before reaching the village."

"What kind of chap?"

"Can't tell you that. I came up behind him and didn't look round."

"Was it unusual to meet a stranger there?"

"Course it was. Well, who is there to be? There's no one much goes up there but the postman, unless it's to the church, and then they'd be in motorcars, or on Sunday when they get a few from the village. With old Rudd dead and buried and Mrs. Rudd not going out much, there was only me and the Neasts likely to be up that way."

"What about the Rector?"

"Well, he does sometimes pop up to the church, but he didn't that afternoon because I saw him as I went through the village after, and he hadn't even got his bicycle with him."

"Are there no other dwellings near the church?"

"There's Hickmansworths, but they don't use that road. Their place lies beyond the church over to the left, but the Potters Cross road runs past them and they don't have to go by Church Lane at all. They fell out with the Neasts years ago and the two lots haven't spoken for I don't know how long. There used to be a cart track between their place and Monk's Farm but it's been Let Go and I doubt if you could find it now. There's a lot of funny people round here."

Carolus looked pained.

"I don't see anything funny about Hickmansworths," said Doll. "I think they're very nice."

Carolus stood up.

"Thank you very much, Mr. Stonegate," he said. "You've been very co-operative. I hope your information will help me to find Duncan Humby."

"It'll make him look pretty silly if you do, after him telling everyone he was the last to see him alive," said Doll.

Stonegate ignored this, and told Carolus grandly he was glad if he'd been any assistance, and he wished him luck.

"You're not by any chance going past the Falstaff, are you?" he asked.

"Yes. I'll give you a lift," said Carolus, who remembered that the landlord of the Falstaff had told him of Stonegate's nightly visit.

"There he goes again." said Doll. "Go and tell that lot up there how you've been interviewed. They've heard it a dozen times but you're sure to tell them all over again."

CHAPTER SEVEN

WHEN THEY REACHED THE Falstaff, Carolus decided to accompany Stonegate to the public bar instead of listening to more of Mr. Sporter's up-to-date phraseology, he soon found that Doll had not exaggerated, for Stonegate entered like a triumphant hero and introduced Carolus to their fellow customers as "one of those who've been to interview me." He seemed to take it as his natural right to have beer bought for him, and with a rather condescending "Well, cheerio" to Carolus, downed the best part of a pint.

One of the two customers was the gnomish little man who had directed Carolus that afternoon, and Stonegate, full of self-importance and benignity, drew him into his monologue.

"Here's a gentleman who ought to be able to tell you something," he said to Carolus. "Being as he lives up Church Lane. His is the only cottage between the village and the farm, as you might say. His name's Puckett if you want to ask him anything."

"I know the gentleman already," said Mr. Puckett, a remark which set Stonegate back for a moment.

Carolus sat down beside the little man after filling his glass.

"What's he mean about my being able to tell you something?" asked Mr. Puckett. "What are you trying to find out about? You're not one of these insurance fellows, are you?"

Carolus took the last question first.

"No. I'm not," he assured Puckett.

"Because I won't have anything to do with them. They got me to insure my wife's life some years ago and as soon as I did it, she died. What do you think of that?"

"Very unfortunate," said Carolus. "You ask what I'm trying to find out about. It's this missing man. He was my solicitor and I'm a friend of his partner and his wife."

"Widow, more likely. You'll never see him alive again, not if those Neasts got hold of him. They're a funny lot."

This was too much for Carolus. This time "funny" had gone too far.

"Funny?" he said sharply. "What's funny about them?"

"Wait till you go up and visit them. You'll see for yourself. No, I don't suppose you'll ever set eyes on that poor fellow again. Not alive, you won't."

"That's a very serious thing to say."

"I mean it serious. I'm sexton up at the church. I pass by their farm every day and never get so much as a 'good morning' because ever since they came here they've fallen out with the Rector and that means me, too."

"What did they fall out about?"

"He's High. They're Low," explained Puckett, "and you can't have it both ways."

"Were you up at the church that Monday afternoon?"

"No. I had a bit to do in my garden. I grow the best parsnips there are hereabouts and even Stonegate here said my sweet peas this year were lovely. As for the asters . . ."

Carolus saw the danger of this diversion. It could last the rest of the evening.

"Can you see the road from your garden?"

"When I'm out in the front I can. But I was at the back that afternoon."

"You don't remember my friend's car passing?"

"There was something passed about half past three," said Puckett. "But I couldn't say what kind of a car it was. It's not my line, you see. If you was to ask me about Michaelmas daisies now I could very likely tell you something you didn't know. But all cars sound alike to me. All cars, that is, except Neast's old lorry. I can always tell that. I should know that anywhere by the sound of it. Sort of a ponkety ponk its got."

"Did that pass that Monday afternoon?"

"I daresay it did about five o'clock when I was just going in to get my tea. Yes, I reckon I heard it. Can't be sure, mind you. I'm so used to it coming by, I can't be certain. But I think it did. I'd been busy with my dahlias. Lovely this year they are."

"Yet you noticed one car and remember the time it passed?"

"Only because I happened to look at my watch just then. I thought that's too early for the Neasts to come home from market. It's a pity I didn't go and have a look over the hedge, but I'm not one to mind other people's business. I saw Stonegate go by on his bicycle though. Must have been about half an hour later."

"Did you speak to him?"

"Just to pass the time of day. 'You're early today,' I told him and he said yes, he wasn't feeling too well. That was all."

"He didn't mention what he had seen?"

"What *had* he seen? That's what I'd like to know. A chap asleep in a car. It's not much to make all this fuss about."

Stonegate heard this from the other side of the room.

"Not unless it's the last time anyone set eyes on the chap," he said severely.

"Ah, but was it? How do you know no one else came down the road after you?"

"They'd have reported it."

"What about the Neasts? They must have gone by?"

"Haven't they told the police they saw the car and didn't stop? They were on their way home and came on the car from behind."

"We're not to know, are we?" said Puckett. "They may have got down from their car and done for him. I wouldn't put it past them. Or someone else might have."

"Pigs might fly," said Stonegate. Carolus felt the conversation was rapidly becoming unprofitable and that he had nothing else to ask for the moment. But yes, one very simple thing. He turned to Puckett.

"Where will I find Dr. Jayboard's house?" he asked.

He had forgotten the little man's proneness to irrelevance when asked for directions.

"Oh, you're going to see the doctor, are you? I don't know what you'll find out from him."

Carolus turned to Stonegate and asked if he would mind telling him. But he had touched on another village animosity, it seemed.

"I don't know anything about it," announced Stonegate. "I have Dr. Lucas from over at Swanwick."

"You'll just about find him at home now," Puckett reflected. "His surgery's six to seven."

"Where is his house?" asked Carolus firmly.

"You know where the Institute is? You don't? Well, go right through the village and when you come to the crossroads, turn to the left past a lot of new council houses. Then up the hill a little way and it's on your right."

Carolus thanked him and ten minutes later was ringing at the door of a nondescript house called Three Beeches. Dr. Jayboard himself came to the door and when Carolus explained that he was a friend of Lance Thomas, he was asked in to a rather shabby sitting-room.

"My wife's away so I hope you'll excuse the muddle," said Jayboard. "I'm no good as a temporary bachelor."

Carolus looked at him. and thought that if he was a contemporary of Lance's he had not worn very well. He looked an elderly man, with a greyish face and thin hair. His clothes were far from new and had never fitted him well; he had a saddened expression and tired but hungry eyes. Not the man one would feel like reminding of "that night at Vine Street" that Lance Thomas remembered.

"I've come to see you, doctor, because I'm trying to trace Duncan Humby. As his disappearance may be connected in some way with Grossiter and the Neasts I thought I had better ask you about that."

"Oh, yes. I see. In what way connected?"

"I frankly don't know yet. But I don't believe in coincidence. Humby had been summoned to Grossiter who had instructed him to make a new will. He was taking it down for the old man's signature. And within twelve hours of each other, Humby disappears and Grossiter dies of what Lance Thomas tells me to call a heart attack. It would take a credulous man to believe that was coincidence."

"I see what you mean. I know nothing about Humby. But I can tell you about Grossiter. It was a perfectly natural death from heart failure. Lance Thomas—we always called him Tom— had attended him for years and knew his condition. He died in his sleep quite peacefully and of natural causes."

"You are sure of that?"

"My dear chap, would I have signed the death certificate if I hadn't been? There is not the smallest doubt of it."

"I'm sure you're right. But it doesn't seem to help much. Could you recall exactly the events of that Monday night?"

"It wasn't Monday night, really. It was early on Tuesday morning. When the telephone woke me, I looked at my clock and saw it was five-twenty. The worst possible time for an emergency call for a doctor."

"It was one of the Neasts?"

"Yes. Holroyd, the elder of the two."

"What exactly did he say?"

"I'll try to remember. 'Could you come up at once, doctor?' Or it may have been 'Please come up immediately.' I asked what's the matter and he said, 'It's my uncle. I think he's had a stroke or something. I think he's dead.'"

"He *thought* he was dead? Didn't he *know*?"

Jayboard, for the first time, smiled—a brief and uneasy smile.

"That really means nothing," he explained. "People *think* their relatives are dead when they call the doctor. It's like saying they've passed on, or they're no more. Perhaps they're afraid the doctor will say that if the person is dead there is nothing he can do, so he's going back to bed. Whatever it is I've noticed that it's invariably used."

"So you agreed to go up?"

"Yes. As soon as I could get dressed. It took less than five minutes. In a district like this, one gets used to night calls. It can't have been much more than half-past five when I reached the bungalow."

"What impression did you get of the two brothers?"

"They seemed alarmed and genuinely distressed, I thought. There was another man there named Darkin. I understood he was Grossiter's manservant. He was more inscrutable—a very reserved type. Holroyd Neast took me into Grossiter's bedroom and I immediately began my examination. I won't give you the technical details of what I found, but if you wish you may have a copy of the notes I made later that morning. There is not the slightest doubt in my mind that Grossiter's death was a natural one. I see no reason to think it had even been hastened in any way. Indeed, in his cardiac condition I am surprised that he had lived so long."

"Thank you very much for those details, doctor. Now there is one point which seems important to me. How long had he been dead?"

"That is difficult to assess. The Neasts told me, and the man Darkin confirmed this, that Grossiter stayed in his room most of each day and was there when the Neasts returned from market. Holroyd Neast went up to him and he was already in bed. His evening meal was taken in to him at eight and at nine Darkin went to take the tray. Holroyd followed him to say good night to his uncle and remained with him some little time. Nothing more was seen or heard of him until five o'clock in the morning when Darkin went in as usual and found him dead."

"As usual? Did he go to Grossiter every morning at five?"

"It appears so. The old man went to bed so early and slept so badly that he was ready for a cup of tea and a biscuit at five."

"Was the bed much disturbed?"

"Not in the least. It seemed that Grossiter had been sleeping peacefully and died without waking up. Not at all unusual in his condition."

"I see. But at what time do you think he died?"

"I can only say that everything was consistent with the times they gave me. Between nine and the small hours of the morning."

"But if you had no information from them at all, would you still have said those were the limits?"

"Not necessarily. The limits are always wide. One of the things that irritates me most about detective novels is the way a doctor glances at a cadaver and says that the man died three and three-quarter hours ago. It is impossible to make such calculations. Had I been judging purely on the condition of the dead man, I would have contented myself by saying he had been dead for more than three hours."

"But how much more? What is your earliest timing?"

"Practically no limit. Twelve hours anyhow, perhaps more. I challenge anyone to be accurate after five hours, say."

"That's not very helpful."

"But why should it matter so much what time Grossiter died? I've told you his death was natural."

"Perhaps you're right. It's just force of habit. One gets in the way of thinking in terms of time with any death. But I'm of course absolutely satisfied with your assurance that death was from natural causes. I know you wouldn't have considered giving a certificate if you had had the remotest doubt. And if there had been any other cause you *would* have had some doubts. So I regard it as Q.E.D. and thank you very much for your information."

"That's all right," said Jayboard.

"You did not see the dead man again?"

"Oh, yes I did. A doctor does not hand out death certificates as easily as you seem to think. I returned later that day—Tuesday—for a final examination."

"What time was that?"

Jayboard smiled. "I can't see how it can possibly matter, but as it happens I can tell you exactly because when I reached the farm, Holroyd Neast was just sitting down to tea and asked me to join him. 'We usually have tea about five,' he said and I glanced at the clock. A few minutes later his brother and the man Darkin came in and to my surprise joined us at table."

"Had you any doubt at all about Grossiter's death to suggest this second examination?"

"Oh, none whatever. It was just to clear up one or two technicalities. I told Holroyd that I was now entirely satisfied and left him the certificate."

"Did he seem relieved?"

"No. He took it as a matter of course."

"Thanks again, doctor."

Jayboard nodded.

"How's old Tom?" he asked, but without much spirit, Carolus thought. They discussed their mutual friends for a few moments before Carolus went back to the Falstaff where he found a reasonably comfortable room.

Next morning he drove back to Newminster and telephoned Thripp at his office.

"What have you found out?" asked the solicitor.

"Nothing directly helpful, I'm afraid. It's a somewhat complicated case, because I am at present going on the assumption, rightly or wrongly, that Grossiter's intended will and his death are directly connected with Duncan's disappearance."

"I'm afraid all that means very little to me," retorted Thripp rather sharply. "What I want to know and what Theodora wants to know is, where *is* Duncan?"

"Of course," said Carolus mildly.

"Have you any reason yet to think he is alive or dead?"

"None yet, I'm afraid. But I daresay the police have. It's more in their line. They'll have examined the ground, and the car for fingerprints and brought all the resources of forensic science to bear. I can only theorise until I discover the explanation that fits *all* the circumstances. I'm not very near that yet. I haven't even seen the Neasts. I'm calling there tomorrow."

"You *do* realise it's urgent, don't you, Deene?"

"Of course. I'm doing all I can as fast as I can."

"Thanks. On my behalf and Theodora's. Now there is a small detail which has occurred to me since I saw you. Have you met the Rector of Hallows End yet?"

"Yes. Whiskins by name."

"Well, Duncan and he were old friends. I knew him quite well, too, though I haven't seen him for some time. Is that in any way helpful?"

"I don't know yet. When were they last in touch, do you know?"

"Duncan sent Whiskins a wire to say he was coming down to Hallows End on business and hoped to call on him. That was telephoned early on Monday morning."

"I only talked to the Rector for a few minutes," said Carolus thoughtfully. "He showed me round his very interesting church. But he made not the slightest reference to Duncan. One would have thought that even in conversation with a stranger, something would crop up. After all, it must have caused a considerable sensation in Hallows End."

"Oh, I don't know. Duncan spoke of him as an unworldly sort of chap. Wrapped up in his church and his responsibilities."

"Unworldly is not the word I would choose for him. But then I scarcely know him. There has been no kind of sequel to that wire? He didn't ring up to say Duncan hadn't arrived, or anything like that?"

"No. Unless Theodora's forgotten it, which isn't likely."

"Do you think he would have known Duncan's car if he saw it?"

"Most unlikely. Duncan's only had that Jag—as he calls it— for about six months, and I should have heard, I think, if he had seen Whiskins in that time."

"Why didn't Duncan telephone Whiskins to say he was coming?"

"That was like Duncan. He used to say that the telephone, which was meant to speed up life and be a convenience, wasted more time than any other invention known to man including the game of bridge. He could dictate a telegram, and his secretary would phone it which took, as he said, two minutes. A conversation with an old friend whom he probably hadn't met for years would go on for a quarter of an hour at least."

"Logical," said Carolus. "This one has, anyway. I'll phone you when I have anything. Goodbye."

As he put the receiver down, Mrs. Stick came into the room.

"He's here again," she said darkly.

"Who?"

"That policeman I told you about. Says it's urgent."

"All right. Show him in, Mrs. Stick."

Carolus lit a cheroot.

CHAPTER EIGHT

"I'M A FRIEND OF John Moore's," said Detective Sergeant Snow.

He was a dapper man, short for a policeman, and he had a warm smile that had been known to beguile people into saying more than they meant to. There was an air of resolve and intelligence about him.

Carolus gave him friendly greetings. John Moore, who had started his career in Newminster, had held the same rank as Snow when Carolus had first known him, but was now a Detective Superintendent and one of the senior men at the Yard. Carolus and he had kept in touch and in two of Moore's highly successful investigations Carolus had been "useful," as the CID man put it.

"Good chap, John," Carolus observed with uncharacteristic heartiness.

"The best," said Snow. "We all like working under him. I've been called in by the local men because this disappearance seems to have ramifications far beyond the village of Hallows End. John Moore suggested I should contact you when he heard that Humby came from Newminster. So I have."

"I'll be as helpful as I can, but frankly it looks far more your cup of tea than mine."

"What do you mean by that, Mr. Deene?"

"If ever there was a case which needs orthodox investigation, this would seem to be it. I've only got a sort of flair for guesswork, you know."

"That's not what the Superintendent says. And in any case you have the advantage of having known Humby before this happened."

"And his wife and partner. But you can make, for instance, fingerprint tests. Any result from these on Humby's car, by the way?"

"Not a sausage. Only Humby's and a garage hand's. But the steering wheel had been wiped clean of them. I think that car was pushed or driven into the side of the road after Stonegate passed it."

"The only people we know who went that way are the Neasts."

"Yes. And in all the circumstances they're natural suspects. But of what?"

"Do you accept that Grossiter died naturally?"

"Not absolutely. Dr. Jayboard *could* be involved."

"A conspiracy? Interrupted by Humby who had to be got rid of?"

"It's just possible on the facts. There's nothing really to support it."

"I haven't seen the Neasts yet."

"That's a pleasure in store for you," said Snow grimly,

"What about Darkin?"

"If there was a conspiracy, he must have been in it. Yet I believe he was sincerely devoted to Grossiter. But all this is pretty wild and unbusinesslike, Mr. Deene. Humby may still be alive."

"He may. But did he *want* to disappear? If so, why? Nothing in his private life suggests it. He seemed to be a happy type, pleased with his physical fitness and so on. Married for thirty years and still good friends, at least, with his wife. Keen on his job, so much so that he had differed with his partner who wanted to sell the practice. It's true he had some money in Switzerland and that he was, possibly by coincidence, carrying his passport that day. But those two circumstances mean very little. And if he wanted to disappear, why on earth should he leave his car at a spot from which he had to walk a mile to the nearest transport under the observation of inquisitive villagers?"

"He may not have disappeared voluntarily, but still he may not be dead."

"That, frankly, seems to me the unlikeliest of all possibilities. How can a man be kept under restraint in England without somebody becoming aware of it?"

"It has been done."

"Not I think, to anyone of Humby's type. Unless there are some very unusual factors here at which we can't even guess."

They had a drink and Carolus said, "Look here. This might not be quite a waste of time. Let's make a list of possibilities, however wildly improbable, to account for the disappearance of Humby. I'll write them down. Don't be limited by common sense, but don't say anything that is not just possible on the facts we know. Agreed?"

The list when they had completed it was a long one:

1. Humby could have lost his memory.
2. Humby may never have left Newminster. His car could have been driven to the spot to which it was known he was going, by someone else who could have been followed by another car in which to travel back.
3. Humby may have deliberately stayed in Newminster and bribed someone to take his car to that point. In that case his object may have been to disappear.

4. Humby may have driven to some other point, like a railway station, and sent the car on as in no. 3. In that case the point could not have been far out of the Newminster-to-Hallows End road because the car had reached Hallows End at soon after four o'clock. In all these possibilities, nos. 2, 3, and 4, Stonegate must either be lying or have seen someone else in the car, but Stonegate's pedestrian could have been the car's driver.

5. Humby may have been prevented from leaving Newminster and murdered there, his car being taken there as in nos. 2, 3 and 4.

6. Humby may have been murdered at Hallows End and his corpse concealed there. In that case, the only people we know of with any sort of motive are the Neasts, or possibly Hickmansworths or Darkin, though it is worth noting that Humby and the Rector were old friends.

7. If Humby was dead when Stonegate saw him, he may have been poisoned before he left Newminster.

8. Humby may have been sleeping when Stonegate saw him. In that case he may have gone voluntarily to the farm with, or before, the Neasts. Grossiter may even have signed his will before the Neasts murdered Humby and destroyed the will. Or Humby may never have reached Grossiter. In that case, why did the car remain in the lane? Or was it driven there later?

9. Humby may have committed suicide. In that case, so convenient to the Neasts, why was his body removed from the car?

10. If no. 2, 5, or 7 is the true explanation, however improbable they seem, the only person *known* to have any motive at all is Thripp.

11. Humby may have been drugged when Stonegate saw him, removed from the car later and murdered. In this highly improbable case, it would seem that either there was some collaboration between someone in Newminster and someone in Hallows End, or Humby was followed by someone from Newminster. Note: he was a fast driver.

12. Humby may have used the opportunity to escape abroad where he had money. In that case his keeping his passport in his pocket was deliberate.

13. Humby may have been murdered *before* Stonegate saw him, either in Newminster or on the way to Hallows End by someone who drove the car to the spot to throw suspicion on the Neasts. In this last case the murderer must have known where Humby was going that afternoon.

14. Humby's car may have been stopped in Church Lane by a car put in the way. In that case obviously the driver must have known that Humby was coming to Monk's Farm that afternoon. But it verges on the absurd to think Humby could have been murdered between three-thirty, the earliest he could have reached there if Thripp is speaking the truth, and four o'clock when Stonegate saw him, if Stonegate is speaking the truth.

"That seems to cover as wide an area as possible," said Snow. "A lot too wide to take seriously."

"Yes, it does. Yet I can't pretend to be madly in love with any of the fourteen points on the information we have. They do suggest checking on a couple of details. Stonegate should be shown a photograph of Humby . . ."

"I've got one," said Snow. "It was on my list of things to do tomorrow."

"Good. I'll cover the other if you like. It is, what time did Humby and Thripp finish lunch at the Crown at Newminster? These points should be easy."

"No need to bother with that. I've checked with both the Crown and Mace's garage. Humby took his car out at one-thirty, as Thripp says."

"Good, and now I think it might also be entertaining and perhaps helpful if we drew up a similar list of Things We Should Like to Know. First and foremost of course would be:

1. Had anyone except the Neasts a motive for preventing Grossiter from making a will?
2. Did Darkin know he was not to benefit by Grossiter's will?
3. Who knew of Humby's intended visit to Hallows End in addition to Thripp and Molly Caplan?
4. Who was the stranger whom Stonegate saw in Church Lane after he had left the car?
5. Did Humby stop anywhere between Newminster and Hallows End? If so, where?
6. Was any other car in Church Lane that afternoon?
7. Where was Darkin all that Monday?
8. Did Grossiter in fact phone Humby on the Sunday morning, as Thripp said?
9. If so, did anyone overhear the call?
10. A three-star question. Was Humby alive or dead when Stonegate saw him in the car?
11. Had Humby drawn any large sum from his English bank account recently?
12. What happened at Monk's Farm to make Grossiter suddenly determine to leave all his money to charities?

13. Where were the Neasts and Darkin on the Sunday morning? At church and chapel respectively?

14. What about Humphrey Spaull? Did he in fact (as it appears) follow Grossiter to Hallows End? Where was he and where was his girlfriend that Monday afternoon and evening? Did he know of his 10,000 pounds?

15. What were the relations between Humby and Molly Caplan? And between Thripp and Molly Caplan? Where was Molly Caplan that Monday?

16. How did Humby's car get from the crown of the road, where Stonegate saw it, to the side of the road where it was found next morning?

17. What did the Neasts do after market?

18. What time did they reach the lane? Had the car already been moved then?

19. Does the family of Hickmansworth, whose land comes right up to the church, know anything at all?

20. Has Puckett told all he knows? His is the only dwelling in Church Lane before Monk's Farm.

21. Was the relationship between Humby and the Rector just auld acquaintance?

22. Did Whiskins tell anyone he was expecting Humby?

23. Or that he had not arrived?

"A nice little lot," said Carolus as they finished. "But they're all really supplementary questions. The main ones remain as they have been from the beginning: One, is Humby alive or dead? Two, where is he or his corpse? Three, did Grossiter die naturally or not?"

"That's about it," said Snow. "Thanks. I will have another. I should like to know what some of my stuffier colleagues would say about me playing parlour games like this, Mr. Deene. Yet, you know, it has clarified my ideas a bit."

"Good."

"The first thing, as you say, is *where is Humby?* Ultimately that's the only thing. It's what we started with and the answer when we find it . . ."

"*If* we find it."

". . . will clear up all the rest. Of course we shall find it. A man can't just disappear and leave no trace."

"It has happened," said Carolus.

"I don't think it could happen today, Mr. Deene. Forensic science has developed fast in the last ten years. We can't prevent crime, but it's not often we fail to find out who is guilty. Besides, there is Interpol."

"I hope you're right. May I clear up one little point on which forensic science will certainly have thrown light? Did you find traces of any activity round Humby's car when your people reached it on the Tuesday morning?"

"That has been one of the most disappointing aspects of the whole thing. There was nothing. Admittedly it rained in the early hours of the morning but even so if anyone had driven over the grass edge, or if there had been any violent struggle some trace would surely have been found of it."

"Thanks," said Carolus. "Now one thing more. I know you must have made a pretty thorough search of the farm and bungalow."

"We have."

"When?"

"On the Thursday. We couldn't have got a search warrant before then. These disappearances, you know—they're so frequent and usually so easily explained that it's hard to take them seriously."

"Did you find anything interesting?"

"Almost nothing. One pair of boots, Cyril's, had traces of the clay which lies under about two foot of soil in that area. But there are places on the Neasts' land where it could have been picked up. Otherwise nothing at all."

They talked cordially for a time and agreed to meet again, possibly at Hallows End, before Snow took his leave.

Next morning at eleven, Carolus set out for Hallows End. He drove from Mace's Garage, intending to time his journey. This could not give him any accurate knowledge of how long Humby had taken to reach the lane but he had travelled with Humby and knew his passion for speed, and by driving a little faster than usual, he could gain some knowledge of Humby's time, provided that Humby did not stop by the way.

The distance was approximately sixty miles over not very fast roads, with a run of about eighteen miles on one of the great motorways. But just after he came through a village called Sneldon, he was thumbed by a young man with a haversack, and decided to give him a lift. The youth accepted this with a nod, and settled down in taciturnity, but the little incident gave Carolus a suggestion which had not yet occurred to him in relation to Humby. Might he not, too, have been thumbed? And by someone expecting him to come this way? Someone who knew his car? Someone who could drive it if Humby was no longer capable of it? Someone who might be identical with the man seen by Stonegate in Church Lane after he had passed Humby's car with Humby asleep in it? Guesswork of course, but it could be interesting.

"Ever been this way before?" he asked his passenger.

"No."

"Making for the coast?"

"No."

"Not very talkative, are you?"

"No."

Carolus desisted and ten miles further on was relieved to hear the hitchhiker say, "Here, please."

Carolus reached the Falstaff just before one, and again lunched there, for he did not wish to reach Monk's Farm till the afternoon, and had time to kill.

Mr. Sporter was glad to see him.

"There's been nothing much doing customer-wise," he said. "It's a bad time of year for us. Our business in the spring and early summer is fab. Falls off in September."

"What about Christmas?" asked Carolus, who never discouraged loquacity.

"Christmas-wise we do pretty well. Oh, by the way, did you see Stonegate?"

"Yes. I gave him a lift here."

"So you did. Only he's in the public bar now. I thought you'd like to know."

Carolus found Stonegate enjoying one of the Farm Fresh Pork Pies advertised on the bar, and washing it down with a pint of bitter.

"Now let's see," he said importantly. "Which was you? Television was it, or the old-fashioned radio? No. I remember now. You're Private Enquiries, aren't you? I've had such a lot of them I can't remember it all. And the police don't hardly give me any peace. There was one along this morning with a picture of the chap I saw in the car to see if I recognised it."

"And did you?

"Course I did. It was him as plain as a pikestaff."

"Mr. Stonegate . . ."

"You're lucky to catch me here. I don't often come up at midday, only Doll's gone over to her friend Frede's at Swanwick. What was it you wanted to know this time?"

"Do you work on Sunday mornings, Mr. Stonegate?"

"Do I work on Sunday mornings? What's that got to do with it? I was the last to see that chap alive. That's what I was."

"I know. I was thinking of something else. You may have other important information without knowing it. I should have said, were you up at Monk's Farm on the Sunday, the day before you found that car in the lane?"

"I was."

"Was everything as usual?"

"Pretty well. Except this chap Darkin went off to chapel in his boss's car."

"Mr. Grossiter had a car at the farm then?"

"Yes. He came in it. It's there now as a matter of fact because this chap Darkin's still up there. Big car, it is. Like a Rolls Royce."

Carolus smiled.

"There's no car *like* a Rolls Royce," he said.

"Then it is a Rolls Royce. This Darkin went off to chapel in his boss's car."

"How do you know?"

"Because the missus was Chapel, and Doll takes after her. I don't hold with it myself. Too much hymn-singing for me, and sermonising. Anyway, Doll was there that morning and she saw him."

"The Neasts were church-goers?"

"Not that morning they weren't. At least Cyril Neast, the younger one, wasn't. His brother drove over to Swanwick where there's a church they favour. Low, it is. They don't like anything High. I saw him go off but the younger one, Cyril, wasn't with him."

"Did you see Cyril again that morning?"

"No. I was busy. But I never saw him go out either, as ten to one I should have if he had of gone."

"One other thing, Mr. Stonegate. That man you saw in the lane after you passed the car. Can you remember anything about him?"

"Ah!" said Stonegate. "They all ask me that. I can see him now. Walking quickly he was. Wearing a raincoat."

"Young or old?"

"I only saw the back of him, remember. I'm not one to turn round and stare. But I should say he was youngish by the way he walked."

"Was he tall?"

"A little on the short side for being what you'd really call tall."

"Stout?"

"Not extra. No, I shouldn't say stout. He wasn't thin, mind you. I can see him now."

"Did you notice whether he was well dressed?"

"You can't tell much from the back, can you? He didn't look down-and-out if that's what you mean. But no more did he look smart."

Carolus gave it up.

Chapter Nine

IT WAS AGAIN A GREY and sullen afternoon when Carolus drove down Church Lane to Monk's Farm. The mile of road with its thick hedges twisted sharply in places so that it was impossible to see far ahead. He passed Puckett's cottage on his right, and in a few minutes stopped his car in the road outside the Neasts' large bungalow.

From the front door to the little wooden gate by the roadside ran a cinder path; nothing grew near it but a few weeds. The gardens of farmhouses were frequently neglected, but this abandoned ground appeared to have been willfully left to waste. No dog barked and the afternoon seemed ugly and silent as the gate clicked behind him and he started to walk to the door.

He had a strong sense of being watched from somewhere. He was familiar with this sensation, knowing that it was apt to touch any man who has to advance towards uncurtained windows through which he cannot see, yet here it seemed particularly strong as though the two brothers were standing out of sight watching his every movement.

This impression was confirmed by the swiftness with which the front door was opened by the elder brother, who stared down at Carolus (himself half an inch less than six foot tall) quite silently but with enquiring eyes.

"Mr. Neast?"

Holroyd nodded.

"I wonder if you could spare me a few minutes. I'm making some enquiries about Duncan Humby."

A lethargic smile appeared on Holroyd's features.

"Certainly," he said. "We are only too glad to give any information we can. Please come in."

The narrow entrance passage of the house had a stale and musty smell. Holroyd opened the first door on the left, and Carolus entered a room which seemed to be both sitting-and dining room. Two men were seated at a large mahogany dining table at which a third chair was pushed back as though Carolus had interrupted a conference of three. The two men rose somewhat awkwardly and Carolus recognised Cyril Neast and the man Darkin. He had last seen them at the crematorium.

"This is Mr. Deene," said Holroyd still with that dreary smile on his long pale face.

"How did you know my name?" asked Carolus sharply.

Holroyd was unmoved.

"We are not quite out of the world here," he said. "And Mr. Darkin comes from Newminster."

"That may be how you knew of me," returned Carolus. "But how did you know I was here?"

"Perhaps Stonegate."

"Stonegate does not know my name."

"Or possibly Mrs. Rudd."

Carolus saw at once that whatever else Holroyd might be, he was not the man to be at a loss for an answer. There was already an air of velled hostility in the room, and Carolus found the atmosphere oppressive and somewhat sinister. Neither Cyril Neast nor Darkin had spoken yet.

"Please sit down," said Holroyd and to Carolus's surprise indicated the fourth chair at the dining table, so that he found himself among them like a fellow conspirator.

The table was covered with a dark-red baize cloth much stained and very worn. In its centre was a painted tin ashtray advertising a hop-spray. The room was unkempt, indeed positively dirty, and the stale smell was as noticeable here as in the hall, unaffected by the tobacco smoke from their three cigarettes.

"Yes," said Holroyd. "We shall be pleased to further your enquiries in any way we can."

Carolus thought that possibly the whole scene had been rehearsed and that two or all of these three men might have agreed on answers to any questions he would put. This was not to say that their answers would be wholly untrue or that they were guilty of anything worse than a little face-saving, but it was extremely uncomfortable and rendered some of his enquiries futile. But truth could appear in ways other than by the spoken word.

He looked about him. A drab and unpleasant room that, it seemed, had never been anything else. There were no pictures on the walls, not even an oleograph, and very little furniture. A settee with a broken spring and covered with imitation leather, a couple of wicker armchairs and a Victorian sideboard were the only sizeable objects in sight. Carolus would have welcomed a merely untidy room, with perhaps a few samples of cereals, a pair of hedge-clippers and a mongrel dog such as he had seen in other bachelor farmhouses. This was frowsy and dull without being picturesque.

Nor did he care for the appearance of the three men, now that he saw them close at hand. Holroyd was thin and tall with thick short hair and a long pale face on which the frequent slow smile seemed a contradiction. He had dirty fingernails and wore old-fashioned shabby clothes. His younger brother was crimson of face and looked like a heavy drinker, with a surly bullying expression. Darkin was no taller than Holroyd but his splay-

ing hands and feet suggested pathological giantism. His large
nose seemed to sniff the air like that of a running camel.

Yes, here in this room by this precious trio almost any conspiracy could have been entered into. Whether any of them was
capable of murder was another matter. Carolus was certain that
none of them was trustworthy, and he could believe any one of
them dangerous.

"Then may I ask my questions as they occur to me?"

"By all means, Mr. Deene."

"Your uncle had been here only six days, I believe?"

He saw Cyril Neast look up. He evidently had not expected
an attack from this quarter.

"That is so. Our uncle's visit was a complete surprise to us.
We received a telephone call on the Tuesday morning—it was
made on my uncle's behalf by Mr. Darkin here—asking if we
could put him up for a night or two. It was the first communication in many years which we had received from him; we were
astonished."

"How did you account for it?"

"After a while the explanation occurred to us. His son and
his son's wife had recently been killed in a car crash in South
Africa. In spite of his quarrel with my uncle, Raymond Grossiter had, we believed, remained his heir. Now the old gentleman wished to see whether he found us worthy to inherit all or
a part of his fortune."

"That was your guess?"

"It has been proved correct by subsequent events. The man
who has disappeared was his lawyer and was actually bringing
him a will to sign."

How easily Holroyd spoke of "the man who has disappeared," how almost genially he gave his account of his uncle's
behaviour.

"But you did not know that at the time?"

"At what time, Mr. Deene?" asked Holroyd severely,

"At the time your uncle proposed himself as your guest."

"As I say, we guessed it was something of the sort. And of course we were pleased and determined to do all we could to make him welcome. A large sum of money is not to be refused by any sensible man, is it? Even if it's only in prospect."

There was something so articulate and professional about Holroyd's way of explaining matters that Carolus asked him whether farming had always been his profession.

"No. I'm a doctor," he said casually.

"You mean you're a fully qualified doctor, Mr. Neast?"

"Yes. I don't practise, however."

"But you are on the register, or whatever it is called?"

"Certainly."

"Then why did you have to call in another doctor when your uncle died?"

"Mr. Deene, surely that must be self-evident. My uncle had a large fortune, and my brother and I were presumably his heirs. Was it not natural that I should want the certificate to be signed by another doctor, and one in whom I had every trust? In my place, wouldn't you have done the same thing?"

"But you knew the cause of death?"

"It was impossible to mistake it. These cardiac cases are really not at all puzzling."

"Dr. Jayboard only confirmed what you yourself had already decided?"

"That is so."

"What did you think about it, Mr. Darkin?"

Darkin cleared his throat.

"I had always known that Mr. Grossiter suffered with his heart," he answered ponderously. "Dr. Thomas himself had told me that something of this kind could be expected, consequently his sudden death was no surprise to me. But still it was a blow, a severe blow. I had been with Mr. Grossiter for seventeen years."

"Did you know that he had made no will?"

There was something a trifle sanctimonious in Darkin's answer. "I never gave a thought to such a thing," he said.

Holroyd spoke genially.

"It seems to me," he said, "that we are getting rather far away from the problem of Mr. Duncan Humby. We are very ready to assist you, Mr. Deene, but I feel I should remind you that you are not investigating my uncle's death, but the disappearance of his solicitor. Unless you connect the two?"

"Not necessarily. All the same I can't investigate one without the other. You have kindly said you will answer my questions. May I have some account of your movements on the Sunday we are discussing?"

"Certainly. Certainly," said Holroyd, his weary bonhommie apparently restored. "Where do you want to start?"

This readiness to give information about himself seemed to Carolus exaggerated and suspicious.

"On the Sunday morning," he said, with a glance at Cyril. "Did any of you go to church?"

Holroyd gave his mirthless leer.

"I did," he said. "My brother, who usually accompanies me, was unable to do so."

"Why was that?" Carolus asked Cyril.

"You ask too many questions, Mr. Deene, about things that don't concern you."

This Carolus thought reasonable.

"I know," he said. "I'm sorry. But I have to get at things my own way."

"Perhaps I had better tell you," said Holroyd, as if to pacify them both. "The truth is Mr. Darkin was particularly anxious to go to chapel and it was impossible for us to leave my uncle alone. You must understand that he had scarcely left his bedroom since he had been with us. I'm afraid our establishment here was a bit rough and ready for him and he preferred the room we had been at pains to prepare. But to leave him with no one to summon in case of need would have been willful neglect and we were not guilty of it. My brother stayed in the house."

"All the time?" Carolus asked Cyril.

"I went along to the farm once to see Stonegate, but couldn't find him."

"What time would that have been?"

"Soon after eleven. I daresay about ten past."

Carolus always found exact knowledge of the time that small things had happened days or weeks earlier, to be somewhat incredible.

"How do you come to remember the time so exactly, Mr. Neast?" he asked.

"Church bells," said Cyril. "They'd just stopped in our church across the way."

"They ring till eleven?"

"This Rector," interrupted Holroyd, "has upset a lot of things with his newfangled nonsense but he has not ventured to change the time of our grand old Eleven O'Clock Service. We don't attend his church ourselves. I'm told it's little better than a Roman Catholic oratory. But we enjoy the peal of bells which is well known around here."

"Were you out for long?" Carolus asked Cyril.

"Not more than half an hour."

"Did you know that your uncle made a telephone call at that time?"

Holroyd joined in again.

"We do *now*," he said. "The police have told us. We had no idea at the time, of course. My uncle was only alone in the house for less than twenty minutes. It must have been then that he telephoned Humby and gave him instructions to draw up a will."

This air of helping Carolus to unravel a mystery was rather beguiling.

"Do you know what were the terms of that will?"

"No. The police declined to tell us that. It was never signed, anyway."

"I wondered whether you knew from any other source?"

For the first time Holroyd seemed a mite disconcerted.

"What other source *could* there be?" he asked.

"You might have enquired from Humby's partner," Carolus said casually.

"We were not sufficiently interested. The will was never signed, so why should we want to know of our uncle's malice?"

"Malice? Then you *do* know that your uncle meant to cut you out?"

"We don't *know*," said Holroyd, "but we think it very likely, all the circumstances considered."

"All what circumstances?"

"You're very sharp, Mr. Deene. I was referring to my uncle's stay here. We are unused to visitors and were not able to make my uncle as comfortable as he liked to be. Nor did he approve of my having given up medicine for farming. And my brother . . ."

A slow grin spread over Cyril's red face.

"I got tight one night and really told him what I thought of him for the way he treated our mother. She was his sister, after all, and he never did a thing for her, the mean old so-and-so."

"I don't think we should speak of him like that," put in Darkin. "I always found him a truly generous man."

"What did he ever do for you?" asked Cyril.

"I did not look for benefits from his service. He paid me well and that was all I asked or expected."

Darkin resembled Chadband more at every moment, Carolus thought. And the resemblance grew when he said, "May I
interrupt with a suggestion? Don't we all deserve a cup of tea?
I can soon make it if you want, Mr. Neast."

"Good idea," said Holroyd. "Go ahead, Mr. Darkin. You
know where everything is."

There was a perceptible relaxation of tension.

"You're giving us a real grilling, Mr. Deene," said Holroyd,
with his unpleasant smile. "The police weren't nearly as thorough as you."

"You're very patient," said Carolus drily.

"We are anxious to be. We are very conscious of being in an
unenviable situation until Humby is found. It is not pleasant to
have someone disappear almost from one's gates, particularly
when that person was on such a mission as Humby was."

"I see that. But I have no official status, you know."

"You have enough for us. We *want* to help. It is in our interest that Humby should be found as soon as possible."

While they waited for tea, Carolus decided to use the break
to discuss a matter outside the range of their discussion hitherto.

"You have recently lost one of your men, I understand," he
said to Holroyd, who on this as on every other subject held the
floor.

"Yes. Most unfortunate. Old Rudd had been with us a good
many years."

"I was interested to hear that you were being so generous in
the matter of his grave."

Holroyd hesitated, then said, "It is the least we could do for
those years of service."

"His widow seems delighted with such an impressive monument as you plan. Are you superstitious, Mr. Neast?"

"I? Superstitious? What an extraordinary question. Not
more than the next man, I believe. Why?"

"The whole business of monuments has always seemed to me somewhat to smack of superstition."

Everybody seemed relieved when at this moment Darkin returned with a tea tray, and in a few moments handed to each of them a large plain cup. A packet of biscuits seemed to have been hastily tumbled out on a plate which was handed round. Nothing more was said for a few moments—the four of them seemed oddly pensive as they drank their tea.

"But you still have a good man in Stonegate?" said Carolus somewhat abruptly.

"A good worker. Not very observant or intelligent, unfortunately."

"I've had a talk with him. He seemed reasonably observant to me, though he could not tell me much about the mysterious stranger he saw ahead of him in Church Lane just after his passing Humby's car."

"Now that *is* interesting," said Holroyd with more animation that he had shown for some time. "Have you any theories about his identity?"

"Not really. I don't often have theories until I can form one simple theory to account for everything. Of course this man may have no connection with what we are investigating."

"He may not," admitted Holroyd—somewhat reluctantly, Carolus thought. "But I can't help thinking he had. Strangers are not often seen in Church Lane on foot. A few motorists want to see the church, but a man walking at that time of the afternoon . . . it's so unlikely."

"You may be right."

Carolus still seemed reluctant to return to what might fairly be called his cross-examination.

"This farm belongs to you, Mr. Neast?"

"To me and my brother. We bought it for a song, I may say. If there's one thing I pride myself on it is being able to seize an

opportunity when I see one. I think it's one of the most important things in life. I saw this going cheap and in a few days had
bought it and thrown up my medical career. That's what I call
decisiveness."

"Very laudable," agreed Carolus.

Holroyd grinned again.

"Now aren't you going to ask us any questions about the
real problem? I mean the disappearance of Humby?"

This time Carolus smiled back.

"I'm coming to that," he said.

Chapter Ten

IT WAS ALL RUNNING too smoothly, Carolus thought, and nearly all Holroyd's answers were too slick to be altogether spontaneous. His willingness to be questioned might argue that his answers had been carefully prepared, might suggest that he had something to conceal, but was by no means incriminating. Yet Carolus was aware of an increasing discomfort in this house that came from more than his hideous surroundings. Whether or not any of these three was a murderer, they were all curious and highly unpleasant people.

So far Carolus had been doing little more than spar with them. The test would come now as he approached the crux of the problem.

"May I once again start by following your movements on that Monday?" he asked as civilly as he could, considering the gross impertinence, in ordinary circumstances, of such a question.

Holroyd was unruffled.

"Certainly," he said.

"My brother and I went as usual to Cashford Market."

"Leaving here at?"

"About eight-thirty."

"Your uncle was still in bed?"

"Oh, yes. He did not get up till midday. He was, as you know, far from well."

"At what time had he been called that morning?"

"At some very early hour by Mr. Darkin," said Holroyd and glanced towards Darkin.

"It was a little later than usual when I went to Mr. Grossiter's room," said Darkin calmly. "Say five forty-five. It was not often I was later than five. Mr. Grossiter felt the need of a little refreshment at this time."

"So you went daily to him, usually at about five?"

"Just so."

"Rather a bore, wasn't it?"

"It was part of my duty," said Darkin unctuously.

Carolus returned to Holroyd.

"Did either you or your brother visit your uncle before you left for market?"

"No. I had told him the previous night that we should be out all day. He had Darkin to look after him."

"And you were out all day?"

For the first time Holroyd seemed surprised and irritated.

"Of course we were. A hundred witnesses at least could be found at Cashford to say that we were there throughout the day."

"You lunched there?"

"At the Bull, where we are well known. We were engaged in business during the afternoon." He became somewhat sarcastic. "I can supply you, if you wish, with the names and addresses of those with whom we dealt."

"Quite unnecessary, Mr. Neast. I expect you have already given them to the police."

Rather dramatically, Holroyd stood up.

"The police confined their questions to matters of interest to them. They were concerned with trying to trace the man who disappeared from here. They did not waste their time and ours with irrelevant questions."

Carolus remained cool and amicable.

"I assure you I should not have been so impertinent as to inquire about your movements if you had not invited me to do so. Perhaps you'd prefer that we broke this discussion off right here?"

Holroyd seemed to be struggling to reach a decision, and his brother spoke for him. He looked hostile and impatient.

"No. Get on with it," he said. "I've got something to do if you haven't."

"Thank you," said Carolus blandly. "I'll be as brief as I can. At what time did you start for home?"

Holroyd seemed to have recovered his equanimity.

"That is the one point of time on which we cannot be precise," he said. "Neither of us happened to look at his watch. But if you were to say five o'clock, or a quarter of an hour more or less, you would not be far wrong."

"And you drove straight home?"

"Yes. There was nothing to delay us."

"Till you reached Church Lane."

At this Carolus fancied there was an increase of tension in the room. Yet Holroyd's voice was casual when he spoke.

"There was nothing to delay us there. We passed a stationary car which we now know to have been Humby's Jaguar."

"Were its lights on?"

"I think not, There was still plenty of daylight. But my brother rather fancies they were. At all events the visibility was still all right and we saw the car as soon as we rounded the bend. "

"But you did not slow down?"

"Oh, yes I did. There was room to pass it, but not more than enough. I had to take it carefully."

"There *was* room? Then it was pulled into the side of the road?"

"Yes. Where it was found next morning. Where the police photographed it."

"That's most interesting, Mr. Neast. Stonegate, who passed the car on his way home an hour or so earlier, says it was right on the crown of the road when he saw it with Humby in it."

"Yes. I know he does. If he is to be believed, and I should think he is, that ties up nicely for you, doesn't it? You have the time, within about an hour, when Humby disappeared."

"No. I have the time when the car was moved. I don't know that this was the same as the time when Humby left or was taken from the car."

"But it seems likely, doesn't it?" persisted Holroyd.

"Was there anyone in the car when you passed it?"

"To tell you the truth, I was so occupied with driving past in that narrow space that I did not notice."

Carolus turned to Cyril Neast.

"Did you notice?" he asked.

Cyril looked surly.

"As a matter of fact I'd had one or two. Market day, you know. I was dozing."

"Yet you noticed that the car's lights were on?"

"I said my brother rather fancied they were," put in Holroyd at once. "I said no more than that."

"So I am to take it that as you both drove home at some unknown time before or after five o'clock you saw in the lane Humby's car which was drawn into the side of the roadway, which may or may not have had its lights on and may or may not have contained a dead or a living man? That's as near as we can get?"

"That's about it," said Holroyd and Cyril grinned.

"Then perhaps Mr. Darkin can help us. Do you remember what time they came in?" asked Carolus.

"I was with Mr. Grossiter," said Darkin. "From his room one does not hear much that goes on in the house and I did not hear either the lorry or Mr. Neast entering. But I noticed when Mr. Holroyd Neast came in to see his uncle. That was at exactly five to six, so they must have been in before that."

Like Holroyd, he was apparently very helpful and like Holroyd he said nothing at all, reflected Carolus. And like Holroyd's, his answers came pat as though they had been well prepared. Perhaps the best chance of hearing something spontaneous would be from the other brother, Cyril. Carolus turned to him.

"Did you see your uncle that evening?" he asked.

"Not I," said Cyril. "I told you I was under the weather, didn't I? Never do for the old man to see me like that."

"What time did you go to bed?"

"How on earth do you expect me to know that?"

"I think I can help there," said Holroyd smugly. "I left my brother in this room when I went to see my uncle at about nine. I was with my uncle for some twenty minutes and when I came back my brother had gone to bed."

"And you yourself followed his example immediately?"

"No. Not for an hour or so. I was reading the evening papers."

"So let's say you went to bed between half past ten and eleven. You heard nothing during the night?"

"Nothing. There was nothing to hear. My uncle died in his sleep."

"And you?" Carolus asked Cyril.

"I was right out. Didn't know a thing."

"Till?"

This seemed to pull him up. Carolus fancied he looked to Holroyd for prompting, but could not be sure of this. He answered after a long pause, "Till my brother came to my room at some unearthly hour of the morning to say my uncle was dead."

"I see. It was Darkin who made the discovery. Would you tell us about that, Darkin?"

"*Mr.* Darkin, please," said the man with ridiculous solemnity. "I was something more than a manservant to the late Mr. Grossiter."

"Oh," said Carolus, preparing to go off at a tangent. "If that is so, and you were his friend, why do you suppose you were not mentioned in his will?"

"I had no reason to suppose I wasn't," said Darkin with a touch of resentment.

"But you know now, surely."

"How . . . how should I know that, Mr. Deene?"

Carolus pressed home his advantage.

"Haven't you seen the will which Mr. Humby had prepared for him?"

"Seen it? Certainly not. How could I possibly have seen it?"

How indeed. Unless from Humby's pocket, thought Carolus. But he said, "There is a copy of it at Humby's office, of course."

Darkin seemed relieved. "I should never have presumed to ask to see that," he said.

Carolus was forming certain fixed conclusions now, about each of the extraordinary persons who confronted him.

"Let's get back to your finding Mr. Grossiter," he said. "It was soon after five o'clock, I believe?"

"Yes. I took him his tea and biscuits as usual. He was always awake at that time, but this morning did not stir. I called him but received no answer. I touched his shoulder and saw at once that he was dead. He was lying on his back quite peacefully. So I went and informed Mr. Neast who called the doctor."

Yes, it all fitted together admirably. There was nothing that any of them had told him that could be nailed as a lie, Carolus thought. There was only one thing that made the whole story improbable—that were it true, there had been one colossal coincidence: Humby's voluntary disappearance on the eve of Grossiter's death. That the lawyer bearing a new will for Grossiter to sign should have chosen to disappear from a spot near Grossiter within a few hours of Grossiter's natural death—that this should have happened by coincidence, was too much for any sane man to believe.

Carolus asked another question. "I suppose the police have made a search of the farm premises?"

"Oh, certainly. And of this house too. We accepted that as a reasonable outcome of events. It was a very thorough one which took four men a whole day."

"Which whole day?"

"Let's see. It was the day before our uncle was cremated. The Thursday, that was it. The day before yesterday, in fact. Things have happened so quickly and strangely here that I'm apt to be confused."

"If I may say so, Mr. Neast, you show very little confusion about anything."

"Ah. I have an orderly mind at most times," said Holroyd.

The room was in semi-darkness now and no attempt was made to light it. Carolus felt its oppressive atmosphere about him like a threat. There was little more he could learn here and he was about to take his leave when to his surprise Holroyd delayed him.

"Now that you have apparently asked us all the questions you want, Mr. Deene, let me tell you something of which you seem to be wholly unaware."

"Could we have a little light on the subject first?" asked Carolus facetiously.

Cyril rose and pushed down a switch that lit one bare bulb over their heads.

"Did you know that my uncle had an illegitimate son?" Holroyd asked.

Carolus rarely admitted complete ignorance of what might be a cardinal fact.

"I had heard some gossip to that effect in Newminster," he said.

"Then you did not know that the young man came on the day after my uncle and has been staying as a lodger with Mrs. Rudd?" persisted Holroyd, with a suggestion of triumph in his voice.

"I did not know exactly that," said Carolus.

"Mr. Darkin was fortunately able to supply us with details of this young man's career. His name is Humphrey Spaull. It appears that his mother, who died some years ago, was house-keeper to my uncle for some years but became pregnant by him some five years before Mr. Darkin took service with him."

"Became his companion," corrected Darkin.

"Exactly. My uncle is believed to have settled a sum of money on Mrs. Spaull but denied all responsibility for her condition. She left his service and bought a small confectioner's shop on the outskirts of Newminster where she brought up her son. He is apparently an athletic young man, now aged twenty-two."

"But what evidence is there that he is Mr. Grossiter's son?"

"My dear Mr. Deene, isn't it obvious? The woman was liv-ing in his house and he provided for her generously. What other explanation can there be?"

"Many. Mr. Grossiter was an eccentric and erratically gen-erous man. If his housekeeper was—to use a phrase of the time—in trouble, he may have wished to help her. Or he may have known who was the father and felt in some way responsible for the situation."

"You may believe that," said Holroyd. "We had not such exalted ideas of our uncle's character."

"You scarcely knew him, I believe."

"That is so. But whatever the truth about Humphrey Spaull's parentage, the point here is surely that he believed himself to be my uncle's son. He came to Hallows End in the hope of seeing his father."

"And did he see him?"

"Unfortunately, yes. We were totally unaware of his identity. We knew that Mrs. Rudd had a lodger, but nothing more. He hung about the place for a couple of days and we thought nothing of it. Mr. Darkin never saw him, unfortunately, or we should have been forewarned. Then one day when my brother and I had business in Cashford and were out in the lorry, the young man waited till Mr. Darkin went for his brief afternoon stroll and broke into the house."

"Broke in?"

"Technically to enter through an unlocked door premises where one has no right to be is to break in, surely? That is what he did. We do not lock up during the daytime and this man Spaull went in by the back door and opened doors till he found my uncle's room."

"What took place?"

"Unfortunately we can only guess. No one knew he was in the house until I myself returned to get something and heard raised voices."

"Raised voices? They were quarrelling then?"

"I heard chiefly my uncle. He sounded furious. 'How dare you come here and threaten me!' he shouted. 'You shall have nothing. Nothing at all. I provided generously for your mother and that is the last I shall do.'"

"And did the young man say nothing?"

"There was a mumble in reply. Nothing articulate."

"And when you entered the room?"

"They both fell silent for a moment, then my uncle said, 'Never let this young man into the house again, Holroyd.' Spaull slunk away."

"Did you see him again?"

"Frequently. He had not the good taste or the good manners to keep away. We saw him, as a matter of fact, leaving the house on the Monday evening, my uncle's last day alive."

"But Darkin was here all day, surely?"

"I was," said Darkin, "But he managed to get in when I was not looking. I found them together."

"This time how were they behaving?"

"Mr. Grossiter lay back on his pillows with his eyes closed. He was deadly white and I thought he had fainted. He raised his hand as if to dismiss young Spaull but said nothing. I quietly led the young man out of the house, then came back to attend to Mr. Grossiter. I gave him a drop of brandy and he recovered somewhat."

"I see. Do you think he could possibly have returned later that evening?"

Everybody seemed doubtful.

"I don't think he could have got into the house without one of us being aware of it. But he might have appeared at my uncle's window."

"Causing the last fatal heart attack?"

"It is possible."

Carolus considered this in silence, then said, "Of course I only have your word, Mr. Neast, that his visits were unwelcome."

Neast gave an unpleasant smile.

"You surely have more than that," he said. "You have seen a copy of that last will my uncle was to have signed. Surely if Humphrey Spaull's visits were welcome, he would have been mentioned in it. It is obvious that he came to Hallows End with that in view. Now, was he in the will?"

Carolus saw that all three men were watching him .

"No," he said, "I'm bound to say he was not."

Holroyd smiled as if to show his satisfaction.

Still Carolus did not move. There was one name which had not been mentioned by either of them, as if by design. Yet Carolus sensed that Holroyd was waiting for it, perhaps with secret anxiety, to come from Carolus.

"Your neighbours here are connections of yours, I believe, Mr. Neast. I mean the Hickmansworths."

"I am glad you use the word 'connections' and not relatives. This is unfortunately another case of illegitimacy which seems to have been frequent in former generations of the family. Gerald Hickmansworth is the natural son of my mother's younger sister."

"So Mr. Grossiter's nephew?"

"My uncle's illegitimate nephew, yes."

"You were not on friendly terms with him, I believe?"

"We had not spoken to each other for several years."

"Your uncle knew he lived here, I suppose?"

"I daresay. He never mentioned him or his brood to us."

"Or to you, Darkin?"

Darkin frowned, perhaps at being addressed without the "Mister."

"Not for a very long time," he said.

"And what about Hickmansworth?" asked Carolus. "Have you any reason to know whether he was aware of your uncle's presence here?"

"It is virtually certain that he did. In a village like this everything is known."

"But he made no effort to see Mr. Grossiter?"

Holroyd looked inscrutable.

"That we know of, none," he said. "He was quick enough to send his son over to see us after my uncle's death. They hoped we knew something about the will, I suppose."

Carolus stood up and thanked them, particularly Holroyd, for their patience and information, then, feeling suddenly rather sick, hurried to the door.

CHAPTER ELEVEN

CAROLUS CAME OUT OF that bungalow as though he were emerging from a region of evil odours, and breathed the fresh air of the evening. He felt that he had been in contact with something poisonous or obscene. Whether any of the three men were guilty of crime or not, he hoped that he would not have to endure their presence again.

He decided to get away from the farm, from the village, from the whole district, at least for tonight and return to the comfort and cleanliness of his own home. No investigation that he had previously undertaken had brought him such a physical reaction as this. He had expected to feet that he was near danger—instead of that there was this cesspool sense of evil. He could see the confident leer of Holroyd even now.

He passed through Hallows End without pausing, but when he came to the main road, he glanced at the car park of the Falstaff and saw something which immediately made him apply his brakes. A blue Ford Consul car stood there alone, looking rather forlorn on the generous space of tarmac supplied by Mr. Sporter for his customers. Carolus turned and drove in, leaving his Bentley near the entrance.

In the saloon bar were Molly Caplan and Lionel Thripp. Carolus greeted them cordially.

"So you found your way here," he said, somewhat ambiguously.

Thripp looked a bit baffled, but Molly was equal to the occasion.

"Thought we might see you, Mr. Deene," she said breezily. "I hope you're on the job?"

"Yes," said Carolus.

"But you'd rather neglected one aspect of it, which is why we've come down."

"Really? What's that?"

"The Rector," said Molly. "We've been to call on him."

Mr. Sporter could not resist this.

"Rector-wise we're pretty well off here, I think," he said. "I like a bit of how d'ye do in church, myself. Candles and vestments and what have you. They say this boy's absolutely coloss at that sort of thing."

"We did not come to discuss ritual with Mr. Whiskins, believe you me," said Molly Caplan. "We came to see him about something very different."

"Perhaps I'm to congratulate you both?" suggested Carolus mischievously.

"Don't be absurd," retorted Molly shortly. "We knew, as you knew, that Mr. Whiskins was expecting Humby to call on him that afternoon or evening."

"And what did you find out? That he didn't call?"

Thripp intervened.

"There's no need to be facetious, Deene," he said. "The information which Mrs. Caplan and I have obtained should be of the greatest value to you. We have established that Humby *did* reach the village that afternoon."

"You have? Well, that's something. It had become pretty certain, you know, when Stonegate recognised his photograph as that of the man he had seen in Humby's car. But Stonegate could have been mistaken or lying. He has a taste for publicity."

"Hasn't he?" said Mr. Sporter. "Publicity-wise there's no one to beat Stonegate. He's terrif, he really is."

"When he wants to be and about certain things," pointed out Carolus. "I don't suppose he's more anxious than the rest of us to throw his whole life open to scrutiny. But that's neither here nor there. What you have obtained, Mrs. Caplan, is badly needed confirmation of his story. I'm grateful to you both. What else did the Rector tell you?"

"He hadn't seen Humby for years, he said," Lionel Thripp replied. "Or me for nearly as long. He used to have a living outside Newminster, and Humby used to go out there. Humby's son, in fact, was one of his acolytes, as he described it. As Morgan Humby is now nearing forty and has been an American citizen for ten years, you can see it was a while ago. But they kept in touch, apparently, and when business brought Humby to this part of the world they were both delighted at the prospect of meeting again."

"Did they meet, though?"

"Not in fact. Mr. Whiskins saw Humby driving through the village and went home to await his coming. As you know he never appeared."

"I don't know," said Carolus. "Did Whiskins say that?"

"He took it for granted we should know that Humby had disappeared from Church Lane and not been seen again," put in Molly Caplan.

Carolus turned to Thripp rather pointedly.

"Tell me, as a matter of interest," he said. "Did Humby include any Hallows End local charities in Grossiter's will?"

"Yes. He did. I don't remember exactly what. The choice was left to him entirely, remember."

"Of course. That was all the Rector had to tell you?"

"I think so. He is very, very upset about the whole thing. Poor fellow seems a bag of nerves."

"He did not give me that impression," said Carolus. "But that was yesterday, and anyway you know him better than I do. Well, I am delighted to have seen you both. I must get back now to the wrath of my housekeeper."

"You suffer from that, too, do you?" put in Sporter, not noticing that his wife had entered the bar behind him.

"Who's a housekeeper?" she asked. "You be careful what you're saying."

Mr. Sporter grinned.

"You're marve, my dear. Absolutely marve."

Carolus left them to it.

Mrs. Stick, as a matter of fact, was delighted to see Carolus back to eat his lapper oh at last.

"I've done it ar long lays," she said. "That's brazy with force meat balls. It's so tender it will melt in your mouth. And I've got a bottle of that wine I told you about, nicely sham bray. So you'll be all right for tonight, anyway, whatever you may get up to tomorrow."

"I'm going to stay at home," said Carolus.

"Well, so you ought, sir, with it being Sunday. I'm sure it must be wrong to go playing about with murders and that on the Sabbath, even if it's not at any other time. I'll bring your dinner in about ten minutes."

Carolus phoned Mr. Gorringer and asked whether he would be at home that evening.

"Mrs. Gorringer and I will be delighted to see you, my dear Deene, at the School House. What time shall we expect you? Nine? Splendid. In the meantime *retournons à nos moutons*."

"Oh, were you having dinner?" said Carolus. "So sorry to disturb you."

At the appointed time he found Mr. Gorringer and his wife in the chintzy drawing room of School House. Mrs. Gorringer was a tall, somewhat scrawny woman with a reputation, fostered by her husband, for wit. Her expression was eager and watchful as though she were forever awaiting a chance to be funny.

"Ah, Deene," said Mr. Gorringer. "Choose your seat and make yourself comfortable. I know you like a good cigar and have reserved for you one of these. Really excellent, I find them. They are called Whiffs and my wife laughingly refers to them as a whiff of grapeshot. You won't? Then a glass of port? No? Perhaps we can tempt you presently to coffee. I hope you bring good news for us? À propos Mr. Humby, I mean. I need scarcely remind you that he is a School Governor."

"I'm afraid not," said Carolus. "In fact I'm pretty certain that Duncan Humby is dead."

Dead?" echoed Mr. Gorringer inevitably, as though he were astounded at the very notion.

"Unless I am wholly mistaken about the whole case."

"And that, I suppose, you will never admit to being. So you will have it that poor Humby is dead. Where, then, is his body?"

"I don't know," said Carolus wearily. "It may never be found. We are up against great cunning and resolve here. It would not surprise me if no one is ever tried, and I certainly doubt if there will be a conviction."

"I will not have that!" said Mr. Gorringer. "You do yourself less than justice. A murderer so subtle that he escapes the net of our Deene? It's not to be thought of." He turned to his wife, "Is it, my dear?"

Mrs. Gorringer seemed to be thinking out a *mot* in reply, but, unsuccessful in her search, made do with a breezy, "Not for a moment."

"I am glad, however, that you have come this evening, Deene, and that for two reasons. One is that I wished to remind you that term starts next Friday so we must hope all your investigations may be completed by then. The other is that I think perhaps—unexpected as this will be to you—I may be able to add my mite to the information you are seeking. That, in modern popular parlance, *shakes* you, I imagine."

"It has not happened before, certainly. What information have you got, Headmaster?"

"Ah! I see I have aroused your curiosity. But it is possible you are already aware of the circumstances. Do you remember, some five years ago, a day boy of the name of Spaull?"

"Can't say I do," said Carolus, "I was never good at the boys' names."

"A pity. A great pity. To know their names is half the battle. However, this boy Spaull will come to your recollection if you remember the last season in which we played Rugby Football before changing over to Association in the Christmas Term and the salubrious game of Hockey in the Spring. Spaull played full-back, a mighty man of valour."

"Indeed? Yes? I scarcely remember the Rugby team."

"I was forgetting," said Mr. Gorringer severely, "your unfortunate attitude of indifference towards the school's prowess in sports. Fortunately I can amend it. Spaull was so over-vigorous in the match against Margate College that there was some rather embittered correspondence between me and the Headmaster of that no doubt excellent institution."

"I remember this Spaull," said Carolus. "An apish lout who failed every exam he went in for, but was excused for this because he played well at some game."

"A flannelled fool at the wicket? Or a muddled oaf at the goal?" asked Mrs. Gorringer brightly.

"Both, so far as I can remember," said Carolus.

Mr. Gorringer showed his displeasure by a long deep rumble as he cleared his throat.

"Spaull," he said, "was School Captain, a dauntless player of Rugby Football and a resourceful bowler of no mean batting ability. He did the school much credit in the field although no great things could be expected from him in the classroom. It now appears, Deene, that he is involved in the events you are investigating."

"How?"

"It has come to my ears," said Mr. Gorringer, and Carolus could not keep his eyes from those hirsute orifices, "that this same Spaull, initial H I believe, was on the scene of the crime when it happened."

"What crime?" asked Carolus.

There was another displeased rumble.

"The crime you are investigating, Deene."

"I wish I knew what that was, let alone where or when it happened."

"Let me then put it that Spaull was staying in Hallows End last week and for all I know is there still."

"He is," said Carolus. "I know that."

"What perhaps you do *not* know, Deene," said the Head-master with triumph in his voice, "is that Rumour has been busy with this young man and has connected him, in no uncertain way, with the late James Grossiter. In a word, he is believed to be Grossiter's illegitimate son."

"Yes. I have heard that tale and I don't believe it for a moment. But his mother was given a handsome settlement when she left Grossiter's service. And Humphrey Spaull was to have received ten thousand pounds from Grossiter."

"I see you are already well informed," said Mr. Gorringer sourly.

"Where you might be helpful to me, Headmaster, is in the matter of Spaull's character as a boy. Did he seem cut out for crime? Would you consider him a potential murderer?"

"Deene, we are chatting informally in the presence of my wife. Nonetheless I must apply all the weight of my office to protest, in the strongest terms, against your suggestion that our system here at Newminster could produce any such ghastly anomaly. No boy who has been in my care will ever, please God, besmirch the good name of the Queen's School by—"

"Not even Priggley?" interrupted Carolus.

"I scarcely regard Priggley as a product of the school at all, remembering his unfortunate background and heredity. But even he . . . However, let me content myself with a simple but emphatic negative to your query. No, sir, Spaull had no criminal tendencies. He was not an intellectual, but an honest, hardworking, hard-playing boy of whom the school may well be proud. And not all your—I use harsh terms perhaps—your perverted ingenuity will succeed in involving him in whatever web of guilt you may be spinning."

"So there!" added Mrs. Gorringer, smiling.

"My dear," reproved her husband. "No one appreciates the felicities of your ready humour more than I, but at the moment I am in deadly earnest."

"Well, thank you for your information, Headmaster." Carolus rose to his feet. "I only came to tell you that I am very pessimistic about this case. I believe Humby is dead, and I doubt if we shall ever get a conviction."

He bade goodnight to both of them and hurried home to bed.

Next morning he realised the soldier's dream and stayed in bed till nearly eleven o'clock, reading the Sunday papers. But just as he was about to get up, Mrs. Stick came to his room, her cheeks flushed and her eyes behind her steel-rimmed spectacles bright and angry.

"It's begun all over again, as I knew it would," she said. "There's two of them downstairs now asking for you urgent about Hallows End and the young man's got his head all bandaged up and looks a sight. I don't like the look of her, either."

"Tell them I'll be down in ten minutes.," said Carolus.

"I was just making my patty mason when the bell went."

"*Perry* Mason, surely Mrs. Stick."

"No, sir, *patty* mason for your first course, and now I don't know how it'll turn out. Sunday morning, too. I told them you didn't believe in playing with murderers on a Sunday but they would have it they must see you at once. Spaull, his name is, and I don't like to ask hers. Not looking like she does."

It was less than ten minutes later when Carolus reached his sitting room and found the couple sitting side by side on a settee. Spaull was burly with a crew cut, the girl was good-looking but somewhat supercilious in expression.

Spaull said at once, as though prompted, "Do you remember me, sir? I was at the Queen's School."

Carolus looked at him. "Yes. I think so. What's the matter with your head?"

"That's what we've come to see you about," said the girl. "My name's Zelia Harris, by the way. Last night . . ."

"Were you there, Miss Harris?"

"Not ecktually."

"Then hadn't we better have the story from Spaull?"

"You're going to get it. We're going to my home to take it down and type it now."

"To *type* it? Why?"

"Tell him, Humphrey."

"It's all rather complicated," said Spaull. "There's a lot of detail I might forget, so Zelia suggested my dictating to her."

"And I said it was the only occasion on which you *would* dictate to me, in any sense of the word."

"Dictating what?" asked Carolus, somewhat impatiently.

"A statement on this whole affair at Hallows End."

"What do you know about it?"

"A good deal more than you think, Mr. Deene," said Zelia. "Humphrey was connected in a certain way with Grossiter."

Carolus turned pointedly to Spaull.

"Do you know anything that may throw light on the disappearance of Duncan Humby?"

Spaull considered.

"I don't quite know. Perhaps you had better read my statement when it's finished."

"But why on earth do you *want* to dictate a statement? If you know anything, why not tell it to the police?"

"I have answered all the questions put by the police perfectly truthfully."

"Then why come to me?"

"Why not?" put in Zelia. "Humphrey remembers you from his schooldays when you were always investigating something. He saw you down at Hallows End the other day, so we put two and two together. I told him to dictate the story. He's not a good raconteur."

"I see. Will you be prepared to answer questions on your statement, Spaull?"

Once again it was Zelia who answered.

"It depends on what they are," she said. "We're not going to be involved in this thing for anybody."

"I certainly see no reason why *you* should be involved, Miss Harris. Indeed I do not see how you come into it at all, or why you have done me the honour of this visit."

Zelia attempted a disarming smile.

"Humphrey's hopeless on his own, Mr. Deene. He's so unpractical. You surely don't mind my giving him a little moral support?"

"Is that what you call it?"

"He has often talked about you. We felt sure you would advise him."

"I will certainly read his statement. But I warn you I may find it my duty to hand it on to Detective Sergeant Snow who is investigating the case."

"Well, if you say so," agreed Zelia.

"I hope it will include details of what took you to Hallows End, Spaull."

"It will begin at the beginning and go on till it comes to the end; then stop," promised Zelia archly, on which they took their leave, promising to deliver the report that same day.

At four o'clock that afternoon, it was handed in a carefully sealed envelope to Mrs. Stick by Spaull who escaped before she could deliver it to Carolus.

Carolus immediately sat down to read it.

Chapter Twelve

Statement of Humphrey Fowler Spaull

WHEN I WAS A SMALL boy I knew nothing, of course, of an irregularity about my parentage. I cannot remember my mother actually saying that my father was dead but it was with this supposition that I reached my teens.

My mother seems in retrospect very young—she was in fact twenty-nine when I was born and died at fifty, two years ago. She was a cheerful person who enjoyed running her successful little business and was popular in the district. She sent me to the Queen's School as a day boy and I became captain of the school teams, both Rugger and Cricket.

At fifteen a woman friend of my mother's told me that I was old Grossiter's natural son, that my mother had been his house-keeper and had been set up in her shop by Grossiter just after I was born. This disturbed and perplexed me a good deal but I did not ask my mother about it. Nor did I ever hear my mother speak of Grossiter except casually as a local character.

I was just twenty when mother died. She had told me that she wanted me to sell the sweet shop after she was gone because there would be enough money then for me to complete my education and fulfill her dearest wish by entering a profession. Her affairs, she said, were in the hands of Mr. Duncan Humby and I should go to him if she died.

I did so a week after my mother's funeral. At first he was civil enough, went into details of selling the shop and told me that apart from this there would be about 2,000 pounds for me from my mother's little estate. Then I made the mistake of telling him the story I had heard about our relations with Grossiter, and he changed his manner in a moment, treating me as though I was a blackmailer. He did not answer my question but said that no good would come of my enquiring into these things, and adopted a rather threatening attitude. "This much is true," he said, "Mr. Grossiter has been extremely kind to your mother who once worked for him. There is nothing more to be said and I hope you will not mention the matter to me or to anyone else again." He became brusque where he had been polite and dismissed me as though I were an undesirable.

This rankled a great deal and I formed a dislike for Humby which I have never lost. It was perhaps his air of authority and well-being which made me think of becoming a solicitor myself. I had never been much good at passing exams but I decided that if I really applied myself I could learn what was necessary about law, and after the sweet shop was sold, I obtained a job as junior clerk with the firm of Dawley, Rowe and Blanchard, who were the chief rivals in Newminster to Merryweather, Priming and Catley, Humby's firm.

The firm, for which I worked happily for a year, had acted for Grossiter at the time when my mother worked for him. I found this out by chance and learned that afterwards there had been some dispute between our then senior partner William Rowe and Grossiter, and Grossiter had taken his business to Humby. It was some weeks before I had an opportunity of looking at the files of that time and I finally did so only about a month ago. The story, when I knew it, surprised me a great deal. I was not Grossiter's bastard son, as I had supposed, but the offspring of his son Raymond Grossiter. When old Grossiter found out about his son and my mother, he was furious and threw both of them out of his house—almost literally, I gathered—though he did not treat them parsimoniously. For my mother he bought the shop, for his son he bought a ticket to South Africa and paid a large sum into a bank for him there. I believe they never so much as corresponded again.

On learning the truth about my parentage, I decided to see old Grossiter myself. I am, after all, his grandson and I felt he should take some interest in the career I had adopted. But I found myself prevented from approaching him by the man Darkin who guarded the house like a trained dog. I tried writing to my grandfather, but receiving no reply, I guessed that my letters were not reaching him. I went to see Mr. Humby, but he told me to leave his office.

The truth was, I wanted to get married to Zelia Harris and I felt that old Grossiter should help me to do so, considering the circumstances of my birth. I was determined to get to see him and eventually—in a pub called the Black Horse—I made the acquaintance of a woman employed in Grossiter's house as a char. She promised to inform me of all that went on and said that if Darkin was going to be absent from the house at any time for long, she would let me know and I could get in.

Before this happened, however, she brought me other news. Grossiter and Darkin were going to Hallows End to stay with Grossiter's nephews and might be there for a week or more.

I saw this as my chance. I asked for and obtained a fortnight's holiday and Zelia drove me to Hallows End. I knew nobody there and thought the best person to see was the Rector. He told me about Mrs. Rudd and I became her lodger. That was on the day after Grossiter had arrived at Monk's Farm—that is to say Saturday, September 11th. I kept out of the way as far as possible, particularly of Darkin, and I am almost certain that for several days he knew nothing of my being in Hallows End.

Rudd died on Wednesday the 15th, and on Thursday afternoon I succeeded in seeing my grandfather. I had noticed that
Darkin usually took a walk in the afternoon in the direction of
the village, and was absent for at least an hour. The brothers, or
one of them, usually remained about the house or farm, but on
that day they had gone out together in their lorry, leaving the
coast clear. I found the back door unlocked and looked into rooms
until I found the one in which Grossiter was dozing on the couch.

He began to fire questions at me. Who was I? What did I
want? Was I anything to do with the Neasts?

I said I supposed I must be in some way related to the Neasts
because they were his nephews. So he said, "Then you're one of
those bloody Hickmansworths, are you?"

I said no, and told him my name.

He stared for a minute, then seemed to relax.

"Bless my soul. Are you indeed? I often wondered what had
become of the child. Milly Spaull's son, eh? Stand in the light. I
want to see you."

He seemed delighted. He asked me what I was doing and
about my schooldays, and a good many questions about my
mother. He took it for granted that I knew whose son I was and
asked if I knew Raymond and his wife had been killed. At last I
got a chance to tell him that I wanted to get married and on
that he began to ask me searching questions about my affairs
and prospects. I answered him frankly and he seemed pleased.

"I'll see what I can do," he said. "Don't count on anything,
though. You're no responsibility of mine, as your mother well
knew. But if I can see my way into helping you to get married I
may very well do it. Who is the girl?"

I told him about Zelia and he asked *what* Harris. I explained
that Zelia's father has a senior position in the Borough Surveyor's
office and he seemed reasonably satisfied. Then suddenly he
said, "How much do you think you need?"

I decided to be bold and said straight out, 10,000 pounds. He looked a bit sour at that, but presently gave a little smile. "You don't mind asking for it, do you? Well, we'll see what we can do. But one thing you can be certain about—you won't be in my will. I've made up my mind to that. No member of my blasted family will be in it. Not one."

He was a vigorous old boy and talked loudly. It seems incredible to me that he should have died of heart failure only a few days later.

We were interrupted by the entrance of Holroyd Neast, a creepy sort of person, I thought. Grossiter seemed to get pleasure in playing me off against the rest of them.

"Where's that blasted Darkin?" he shouted at Holroyd Neast. "This young man's been prevented from coming to see me when he had every right to do so. You hear that? Every right! D'you know anything about it?"

Neast's ugly grin disappeared.

"No," he said. "I have never seen this young man."

That was a lie, to begin with. I'd run into him that very morning.

"Well, Darkin has, and deliberately prevented him from seeing me."

Darkin came into the room at this minute.

"You'll be sorry for this," the old man shouted. "I know very well why you tried to prevent him seeing me and you've *exactly* defeated your own purpose. I'll see to that. You'll soon know where *you* stand. What about his letters? He says he has written half a dozen times. Why have I never received his letters?"

"You have always received every letter that has come for you, Mr. Grossiter," said Darkin.

"Lies. Lies. But you've done yourself no good by this. You'll find that out one day. Now bring me my tea, you ape. Don't stand gibbering there!"

He gave me his hand.

"Come and see me again," he said. "And I'll see what I can do."

I walked out feeling as though I was escaping from a snake pit.

I did not go to see him again until early on the Monday afternoon—his last afternoon, as it transpired. I knew the Neasts were out because Mrs. Rudd said they always went to market on Mondays, but I thought Darkin was in the house. I went to the front door, rang the bell and asked to see Mr. Grossiter. He went away to ask, then showed me in.

But the old man was in a very different mood and seemed suspicious about something

"What made you come this afternoon?" he said.

No particular reason, I told him.

"Damned funny you should choose today. I told you you wouldn't be in my will, didn't I? Well, you won't. Not you or any of them. So it's no good trying to make me change my mind at the last moment."

I have wondered since what he meant by that and suppose it was because he was expecting his solicitor that afternoon.

"I may or may not have done something else for you, but it's no good looking for that. The terms are all settled."

He waved his hand as though he wanted me to go, and I thought it best to leave. Darkin was grinning when I passed him in the passage.

When I came out of the bungalow, it was about half-past three and I decided to walk to the village before returning to Mrs. Rudd's for tea. I did not go by Church Lane, but took the footpath which runs from the church and cuts off the main curve of Church Lane, joining it near the village at a point opposite to Puckett's cottage. Had I followed the road, my evidence might be more valuable now for I should've passed Humby's car or seen him driving towards me. As it was, the only human being I saw between the church and the village came up behind and passed me on a bicycle just after I had joined Church Lane. I did not know the man then and he did not turn round to look at me, but I know now it was Stonegate, cycling home early because he was unwell.

After tea I went out again, and standing near the church-yard I heard the Neasts' lorry coming up the road, and out of sheer curiosity watched. Holroyd Neast was driving it and stopped for a moment at the gate of the bungalow. He got out there and went in while Cyril Neast took over the wheel and came on to the farmyard. He put the lorry in the barn where they always keep it, locked the barn door and walked back to the bungalow. I went back to Mrs. Rudd's.

I went to bed early that night. I sleep very lightly and some time later was awakened by a light flashing across my eyes. I knew what it was, for it had happened once before. A car with headlights was coming up the lane and turning into the farm-yard. Just as it turns in the gate its lights just catch the windows of this cottage. I got up and looked out, but I heard and saw nothing. I looked at my watch and saw it was twenty past twelve. I thought nothing of it at the time.

Perhaps Cyril had been out on the booze and was putting the lorry away. But when I heard afterwards what had hap-pened during the night, I remembered it.

I kept away from the bungalow on the Tuesday, though I heard Grossiter was dead. On Wednesday morning I decided to go over there and ask to see my grandfather before he was put in his coffin. It seemed the least I could do because whether or not he had done anything for me, he had intended to, and I was grateful for that.

Darkin opened the door and I told him what I wanted. He was not actually rude, but took a very superior attitude. He would see, he said, and closed the door on me.

Presently Holroyd came out. He had that smile of his on his face but he did not look friendly.

"You realise, don't you, that your intrusion on my uncle the day before yesterday may have brought on his last fatal heart attack?"

I said I realised nothing of the sort. As a relation I demanded to see the body.

"I have no right to exclude you from that, though if you had the least respect for him I think you would keep away. However, I shall not judge you. It is not convenient for you to come in now, but the undertaker is not coming until this afternoon. If you come here at about twelve o'clock you will be admitted to the room for a moment or two."

He then shut the door on me. I went back at noon and was duly shown my grandfather's body. He looked quite peaceful. There was only one thing I thought rather odd about him. He had shaved his moustache—or it had been shaved off after his death. This seemed to improve him, and in death he looked a kindly and benign person rather than the irritable old gentleman I had known.

I did not go to the cremation. Zelia couldn't come down to take me and I had no car. Nothing else happened worth recording, in fact, until last night—the night of Saturday, September 25th.

It was to be my last night in Hallows End. Zelia was coming down very early today, Sunday, to take me back to Newminster in time for lunch so that I could return to work on Monday morning. I went up to my room at about ten o'clock and sat working at some law books I had brought with me, for rather more than an hour, I think. Then I went to bed and slept for some time—I don't know how long.

I woke suddenly. I do not know what woke me—some noise or light, I supposed. I sat up in bed, fully awake and alert, listening. I could hear nothing, yet I was convinced that there was something to hear. I can't explain this; I can only say that the silence did not seem natural. I decided to dress and go out.

From the window I saw that a heavy mist hung over the churchyard, almost a fog. I stood there without turning on the light for some minutes, then I thought I heard, distantly through the mist, the sound of digging. It was an eerie sound to hear from a churchyard in the thick darkness of the night.

I dressed in the darkness and very cautiously opened my door. There was another sound audible in the passage, the regular snoring breath of Mrs. Rudd in her room next door to mine. I started to creep downstairs with my shoes in my hand. I reached the front door and very slowly and quietly began to unbar it. I could hear Mrs. Rudd continuing undisturbed above me. I thought I would be able to get out without disturbing her, but just as I was closing it the front door seemed to swing to of its own accord. I had forgotten it had this habit. It seemed to make a loud bang in that silence and I remained where I was, quite motionless and hidden in the porch, for some minutes to see whether Mrs. Rudd would wake and come down. There was not a sound from the cottage, so I concluded she had failed to wake.

I put on my shoes and made for the front gate, then came round to the entrance to the churchyard. I stopped here and listened again. Now I was sure of it—a sound of digging almost as steady and regular as Mrs. Rudd's snores.

But no light was to be seen anywhere. That was the uncanny part. Two men, I thought by the double spade movements, were digging away somewhere in the churchyard in complete darkness.

Very cautiously, I opened the lych gate and began advancing towards the point from which I thought the sound was coming. As I did so I realised that this was the place where old Harold Rudd had been buried a week ago.

At first I had the absurd idea that this was something to do with the memorial stone which was to go over his grave. I soon dismissed that. Memorial masons don't deliver their handiwork at midnight and work to set it up without a light. Then what was it? I took a step forward, then suddenly felt a blinding blow on the back of the head. Or did I feel it? I scarcely know if you could call it feeling because it knocked me completely out. Yet somehow in the second before I lost consciousness I knew that this had come from behind me.

The next thing I knew was that I was lying in excruciating pain and deathly cold on a gravel path in the churchyard with the first streaks of dawn above me. I tried to move, but it was a long time before I could do so. Then I staggered across to the cottage and upstairs, knocking on Mrs. Rudd's door.

She at once called Dr. Jayboard. When he came he cleaned and bound up a wound on the back of my head without asking any questions. Then he enquired how it happened. Some instinct told me not to tell him the truth and I made up a story about coming home after a drink and slipping to crack my head on a gravestone. He seemed to accept this and told me I had had a lucky escape. There was no sign of concussion, he said, and except for a severe headache which I still have, I rapidly began to feel better.

At eight o'clock, while I was having my breakfast, Holroyd Neast came to the cottage and asked to see me. "I hear you've had a nasty accident," he said. "How did it happen?"

I told him I had gone out the night before and must have slipped and cracked my head, for I remembered nothing till I came to in the churchyard. He said he was very sorry and asked if there was anything I wanted. He sounded friendly and I thanked him.

When Zelia arrived soon after, I told her what had happened and she suggested that as soon as we reached her home I should dictate to her the whole story so that I could make a businesslike report. It was she who realised that what I knew might be important in the matter of Humby's disappearance. So I agreed to do as she asked.

By nine o'clock I felt well enough to return to Newminster with Zelia and it was on the way up that we decided to bring this report to you as you would know best what to do about it. So here it is. If you think the police should have it, please take it to them. To the best of my knowledge and belief it is strictly true in every detail.

Chapter Thirteen

As Carolus reached the end of Spaull's statement, he looked at his watch. It was 4:35. He stuffed the sheets into his pocket and without waiting to tell Mrs. Stick he was going out, slammed the front door after him. He was out of the town on the road that he had come to know well by which he would reach Hallows End in a little less than an hour and a half of fast driving.

He was engaged in a race—not directly with any human force, but with light. Something had to be done by natural light before the late September evening closed down too far. This was his instant reaction to his reading of Spaull's story.

He passed the Falstaff Hotel at a little before six o'clock, and slowed down for the winding road to Hallows End. He turned down Church Lane and stopped at the tiny cottage of the gnome-like Puckett. He had already been forced to use his car lights and knew that there was barely time for his purpose. Yet he knew that it would be impossible to hurry Puckett over his divinations without antagonising him. When Puckett opened the door, Carolus appeared to be breathless with the urgency of the moment.

"Oh, Mr. Puckett," he said. "Could you possibly come with me for a few moments? It's rather urgent."

"What's rather urgent?"

"I want to show you something before the light goes."

"Show *me* something? I don't know what you want to show me. There was a naxident up there last night."

"I know. It is as a result of that . . ."

"Something to do with those Neasts. Must be. Though it wasn't their car that went up and down the road last night, that I do know."

"Mr. Puckett . . ."

"I don't know why you come to me. I don't know anything about it all. Where do you want to go?"

"I'll tell you that as we go along."

"Yes, but go along where? Is it a long way?"

"No. No. You'll be back here in fifteen minutes."

"Not going for a long drive, then?"

"No."

"Because I've often wanted to take a ride in a car like that one of yours."

"Afterwards, if you like. If you'll come now, straightaway."

"Oh, I don't say this evening. One of these days I'd like to, though. I'd like to get back soon if I'm coming with you. In fact, you better leave me up at the church afterwards. It'll be time for Evening Service. There's not many comes nowadays but I have to be there."

"I'm afraid it will be too late if we don't go soon."

"Too late for Service? I don't see how it can be. Fifteen minutes, you said, and Service doesn't start till six-thirty."

"I'll certainly leave you at the church, only could you come now?"

"I've got to get my coat on, haven't I? Can't go traipsing about the place like I am now. Wait a minute, then, and I'll get ready."

Puckett's preparations did not take long. He was wordy but not slow-moving.

In the car Carolus hurriedly explained.

"I want you to come and look at Harold Rudd's grave. I rather think it may have been disturbed."

This seemed to shock Puckett into a silence from which he had not recovered when they reached the lych gate. Puckett almost jumped from the car and led the way across the church-yard to an earthy mound over which nothing had yet grown. This he began to examine from all angles, squinting and moving about like a terrier.

"I don't know whether Rudd's been disturbed or not," he said at last. "But this grave is not how I left it."

"You mean?"

"I couldn't say whether it's all been dug up right down to the coffin, but someone's had some of it off the top and put it back again, that's certain. Look at all this clay over the grass here. I should never have left that, and besides it has rained heavy since we buried Rudd to wash that all away if I had of done."

"You're sure someone has been digging here, then?"

"Of course I'm sure. I've got to go over to the church now, but I'll tell you what I mean later if you like to wait till after Service. If there's only him and me the Rector won't go through with it, not Evening Service that is, though if it was what he calls Marss in the morning there's nothing would stop him. So I may be free as soon as I've put the lights out or I may be half an hour or so, because we can't have hymns if there's only two or three of us, can we?"

Carolus waited for a few minutes before driving away, but when he saw a station wagon draw up, and five people leave it to enter the church, he knew that Puckett would be occupied for at least thirty minutes. The five—three men and two women—Carolus had not seen before and he wondered vaguely who they might be. But he passed several more pedestrians, apparently bound for the church, as he drove towards the village. The Rector would have quite a congregation this evening.

He parked his car in the village square and, finding the telephone booth there empty, went in and after some delay got through to Snow's home. The Detective Sergeant did not sound in the least peeved at being disturbed on a Sunday evening and greeted Carolus amicably.

Carolus came at once to the point.

"Do you think you could get an exhumation order for Harold Rudd's grave?" he asked.

"Rudd? That's the man who was buried on the Saturday before Humby's disappearance, isn't it? But he died in hospital."

"Yes, I know. But I've reason to think his grave was disturbed last night. Young Spaull . . ."

"We know all about him now."

"Yes. He has made a long written statement to me. I shall of course hand it to you at once. I told him he should have reported to you. This gave me reason to think that Rudd's grave had been interfered with and since then I've confirmed it."

"I shall have to find out the legal position, Mr. Deene. It may be more difficult than one would suppose. We can have no reason connected with Rudd himself for exhuming."

"I leave that to you. I'm sure you can manage it. When you hear everything from me I think you'll see it's necessary."

"When will that be, Mr, Deene?"

"I am staying down here tonight."

"Tomorrow morning, then. I'll make this application and come straight down. You'll stay at the Falstaff, I suppose."

When Carolus returned to the church the service was over, but by the light in the church porch he saw the Rector with Puckett. The Rector recognised him.

But he was not the same cheerful man that he had been on Friday afternoon when he had shown Carolus the church. He seemed now hesitant and nervy and all the heartiness had gone from his manner.

"Yes," he said to Carolus. "I remember. You were interested in church architecture. I'm afraid now I have to . . . I'm expected . . ."

"I'm delighted to have run into you, Mr. Whiskins. You see, I'm investigating the disappearance of Duncan Humby. I understand he was a friend of yours."

"Oh, you are? I had no idea. A friend? I hadn't seen him for many years. I really knew his partner better."

"Yet you were able to recognise him in his motor car last Monday."

"Last Monday? Certainly not. I did not recognise him. I doubt if I could do so after so many years."

"Yet you told Mrs. Caplan and Mr. Thripp that you had seen him in the village."

"No, indeed. That is not at all what I said. I told Mrs. Caplan about this large black car I had seen turning up Church Lane, and she said at once it must have been Humby's. She seemed convinced of it, as though she wished me to have recognised him. But all I described, or could describe, was the car."

"I see. Then there is still nothing but Stonegate's word to tell us that Humby was in the village."

The Rector blinked.

"You mean that? It may be that our little community here is not connected with his disappearance? I should be so delighted. But I don't see why Stonegate should lie."

"Nor do I, yet."

Carolus watched the Rector laboriously lighting his bicycle lamp.

"You don't use a car?" he asked casually.

"Not for some years. My predecessor here, Canon Spotter, was killed in a car accident and when I first came, I felt that people might prefer I should not drive. So I took to bicycling and now prefer it. Healthier, altogether."

He nodded to Carolus, wheeled his cycle out to the road, mounted and cycled slowly away.

Carolus turned to Puckett, who had waited patiently.

"I wanted to ask you about something you said at your house. Speaking of the Neasts you said it wasn't their car that went up and down the road last night."

A look of rustic cunning came over the wizened features of the little man.

"The Falstaff will be opening about now," he said. "I don't often go to the Ploughman in the village. They've got new people there I don't take to much."

Carolus took the hint.

"Get in," he said. "I have to go up to the Falstaff in any case. You can tell me about it there."

"As for Stonegate being a liar, I shouldn't put it past him," said Puckett as they drove through Hallows End. "Him and Rudd weren't very friendly, you know. He was a bit too thick with those Neasts for Rudd's liking. Or for mine, for that matter."

They reached the Falstaff and Carolus led the way into the public bar, hoping to avoid Mr. Sporter's peculiar idiom, at least until he had heard what he wanted from Puckett. The sight of a pint seemed to cheer the little man, and instead of making his usual circuitous approach to information, he began straight-away.

"Yes. Last night," he said. "I don't know what made me notice. I did slip in to the Ploughman, as a matter of fact. I don't often go there, as I told you, only it was Saturday night. I came away early. About an hour before closing. And on my way home

I met Cyril Neast hurrying up the lane on foot. I knew what that meant. He was going to get properly boozed. When he's like that, his brother won't let him take the car and he has to walk up to the Ploughman. When he's bad enough they call Mr. Hedge, who has a taxi in the village, to run him home. Other times, if he can walk he does. I've seen him stagger past my cottage as late as midnight sometimes because he Gets it Round the Back."

"Did you see or hear him returning last night?"

"No. I didn't. Unless he was in this car I heard go by. The one I was telling you about. What time it was I couldn't say but it went past as though it was going up to the farm. Then about an hour later it came back again and that's the last I heard of it. All I can tell you it wasn't Neasts' old lorry. I know the sound of that."

"Was it Mr. Hedge's taxi though?"

"No. It wasn't. Mr. Hedge brought a party up to the church this morning and I asked him. No, he said, he hadn't been called out at all yesterday. Nor last night. So it wasn't him."

"You've no idea at all who it might have been?"

"Not to speak of, really. Only, you saw that party came to church this evening? Five of them, there was. It did just crost my mind. No reason for it, mind you. Those were the Hickmansworths from the farm up the other lane. Their ground joins on to Neasts's but there's no way across. They have to come all the way round by the lane. What made me wonder is they're supposed to be some sort of relations of the Neasts, only they haven't Spoken for I don't know how many years, until just recently."

"You mean they've made it up with the Neasts?"

"That's what it looks like. Their car was up there the other day anyhow, outside the bungalow, because I saw it when I went to lock up the church."

They were interrupted by the entrance of Stonegate who, seeing them seated together, gave a curt nod and went to the farther side of the room. But Puckett seemed almost as uncomfortable as the bigger man and after a few minutes said, "There's a bus runs into Hallows End at eight-five and I think I'll catch it. Save you driving all that way. No, thanks all the same. I must be getting along." He hurried from the bar.

Stonegate looked up.

"I don't know what he thinks he might have to tell you," he said.

Carolus decided to play this up.

"Oh, he gets about," he said.

"He never even saw that car that afternoon."

"No, but he heard one last night."

Stonegate looked up sharply.

"What's last night got to do with it? No one disappeared last night, did they?"

"Not that I know of. From here, at any rate. Can you drive a car, Stonegate?"

"Can I drive a car? Of course I can. I shouldn't like to say how often I've driven Mr. Neast's. And a tractor. What makes you ask that?"

"Curiosity," said Carolus. "Do you know the Hickmansworths?"

"No. And I don't want to. I suppose you're going to say they've seen something, too?"

"I don't know. I haven't met them yet."

"They're a funny lot," reflected Stonegate.

Carolus winced.

"In what way?"

"I shouldn't like to say," replied Stonegate, "They keep themselves to themselves," he added.

Carolus went through to the saloon bar to see Mr. Sporter about his night's accommodation.

"You're still around then?" said the landlord. "Pretty persis, aren't you? I suppose you have to be, investigation-wise."

There was a welcome pause while he poured Carolus's drink. Then he came out with a casual remark which Carolus found shattering,

"I hear they're going to dig someone up tomorrow," he said.

"You hear *what?*"

"An exhumation laid on. Gallup, the copper from Hallows End, was in just now. Off duty, of course. He told me he'd been told to lay on a couple of men for it tomorrow afternoon. It isn't certain yet but he's to have these men ready to dig. Casual labour, of course. Pretty grues, isn't it? I've never come across anything exhumation-wise before."

Carolus made a mental note to get Gallup reprimanded for opening his mouth.

"When had he heard this?" he asked Sporter.

"Just before coming here, I gathered."

"Anyone hear him tell you?"

"No. Only the wife, and she wouldn't say anything."

What was the good? He knew enough of small communities to guess that once spoken, information like that could spread to the farthest outlying cottage in half an hour.

There was only one thing to be done. He said nothing, but at closing time went up to his room, provided himself with a couple of blankets and a supply of cheroots. He dare not even ask Sporter for a thermos flask, but, after putting the blankets in his car unobserved, told the landlord he had to drive over to Cashford and would be back about midnight. Mr. Sporter gave him a key.

Chapter Fourteen

CAROLUS WOULD HAVE LIKED to leave his car there in the car park, but it was essential, he thought, that Sporter and anyone else who might be watching should think he had driven away towards Cashford. But when he reached Church Lane, he felt it safe to take the direction he wanted. He remembered that there was a derelict barn a little way down on the left and in the shadow of this he left the Bentley.

He wished, as he continued on foot towards Monk's Farm, that he knew the route of Spaull's footpath, but decided he could not risk going astray tonight. His senses were alert and he paused occasionally to listen. It seemed that nothing disturbed the calm of that late September. The weather was cold and there were patches of mist over the fields, but the moon shone fitfully and at times Carolus could see the stars.

As he approached the Neasts' bungalow he walked more cautiously, his feet going through the grass of the verge silently and he himself lost in the shadow of the wayside trees. Thus he passed the house, noting that there were no lights visible.

When he approached the churchyard, he saw that the general darkness was broken by a sharp light in one of Mrs. Rudd's upper windows. But this went out just as Carolus had passed in through the lych gate and taken his way towards the porch. There he put down his blankets and, always keeping in shadow and on grass, went to Rudd's grave—which so far as he could see, was as he had left it that afternoon. At last he settled in the church porch with his two blankets round him.

Carolus had a trick of dozing like a cat with all his senses enough awake to bring him into instant consciousness at the slightest thing. He remained thus for nearly an hour, until the silence was broken by a sound which he instantly recognised as the closing of Mrs. Rudd's door. So last night, someone, waiting where he was now, might have heard the door slam when Spaull emerged, and been prepared later to approach him from behind and deal that skilful blow which had made him unconscious.

Now footsteps approached, slow and a little faltering, of someone who carried no light and was not sure of the way through the ground mist that was heavy just then in the churchyard. Carolus stood perfectly still and waited.

Then there was a shadow in the entrance of the porch.

"I thought I saw someone come in here," said Mrs. Rudd. "It's a good thing I've got cat's eyes, as my husband used to say, and can see better than others at night. I was keeping an eye open, though, after what happened last night. Now I know it's you, it's all right."

Carolus wondered why he should be given this spontaneous trust. Perhaps Spaull had spoken of him.

"I wish you'd been here last night," went on Mrs. Rudd. "You wouldn't have let yourself be knocked on the head like that. Of course I knew at once what it was when that poor young man came staggering into the cottage, but he *would* have it he'd slipped and fallen over backwards. So I let him say it. If the doctor liked to believe it, that was his business, though I thought Dr. Jayboard looked as though he knew more than he said."

Carolus could see now that Mrs. Rudd was hugging a large shawl around her. She did not seem in a hurry to return to her cottage.

"Do you think they'll come again, then? Is that why you're out here tonight?"

"Who?" asked Carolus.

"Those who were at my husband's grave last night. Oh, I know all about it. Mr. Puckett told me at church tonight. Besides, it wasn't the first time."

"What do you mean?" asked Carolus quickly.

"What I say. They tried once before."

"You mean that someone interfered with your husband's grave before last night?"

"Certainly that's what I mean. It was last Wednesday. Mr. Spaull had gone to see his young lady and I was alone in the house, when all of a sudden I woke up and looked out of the window. What made me do it I don't know. Instink, very likely. Anyway I saw a light over by my husband's grave."

"A light?"

"Yes. Not much of one. Not enough to let me see who it was or how many of them there were. They must have heard me open the window because I could hear them shovelling back the earth as fast as they could."

"Shovelling it back?"

"That's what it sounded like. They'd got the wind up, see? Perhaps they didn't know Mr. Spaull was away and thought he'd be after them. So I shouted out, 'Hey! What are you up to over there?' I saw the light moving away in a hurry then. I'd have gone out if they hadn't. I wouldn't have minded how many there were if they was going to upset my old man's grave. But I didn't need to. They were off, light and all. I knew what they were after."

"You did?"

"Yes. The dirty thieving lot. See, I'd put my old man's gold watch in with him. It was a silly thing to do, I know, but it didn't seem like him without it. He'd worn it all his life ever since he'd courted me. His mother gave it him after his father died. It was real gold and worth I don't know how much. He'd had ever so many offers for it."

"But how would anyone know it was in the coffin?"

"You don't know these parts. There's nothing that isn't known within five minutes of it happening."

"Did you report it?"

"I told Gallup, the policeman in the village, and he came out and had a look. All the flowers had been put back and it looked just as it was left after the funeral, so he said I'd been imagining things. I let it go at that. What's the use with anyone like Gallup?"

"Did you tell Spaull about it when he returned?"

"No. I didn't bother. It's no good upsetting anyone, is it, and he was such a quiet young man. Anyway, you can see I was right about that lot because they came back last night and from all accounts this time they got what they wanted."

"You will soon know, Mrs. Rudd. I told the police what happened last night, and Puckett's belief that the grave has been disturbed, and they're getting an exhumation order. But I don't think you'll find your husband's coffin has been opened."

"I hope not, anyway. It seems a shame if someone can't have a bit of peace once they're dead."

They stood in silence for a moment. Nothing was audible around them.

"Are you going to stop here all night?" asked Mrs. Rudd. "If so, I'll go and make you a drop of nice hot tea."

"No, thanks. After what you've told me there's no need to stay. I wish that idiot Gallup had reported this business when it happened."

"Didn't he, then?"

"It seems not. If he had done so . . . However, you go back home, Mrs. Rudd. You'll see tomorrow that your husband has not been disturbed, I think."

"Well, that'll be something. Only it's very upsetting, all this, when someone's Gone. I wish I'd kept that watch now. It isn't as though it could be any good to him. You don't know what to do for the best, do you?"

"Not always," admitted Carolus, and set off on foot for the place where he had left his car. Still the windows of the Neasts' bungalow were black. Nor was any light visible in the Falstaff when he reached it. He let himself in and secured a few hours' sleep.

Next morning he had to wait till Snow came, and this made him angrily impatient. At this point in his investigation speed seemed important to him and he knew exactly what he must do next.

When Snow arrived, Carolus gave him Spaull's report and told him briefly of Puckett's certainty that the grave had been disturbed, but did not mention Gallup's failure to report what Mrs. Rudd had told him. He had already complained of Gallup's indiscretion about the exhumation, for that was a breach of security for which any policeman should be reprimanded. But this was natural stupidity and he saw no reason to damage Gallup's career for that.

When, however, Snow asked him, after reading Spaull's report, what he expected to find in Rudd's grave, he curtly said "Rudd," and left Snow to draw his own conclusions. He had a job to do now and it was an important one. He was gong to see the Hickmansworths.

Of this family he knew only five facts. One, that they were reputed to "keep themselves to themselves." Two, that they were illegitimate cousins of the Neasts. Three, that it had originally been through them that the Neasts had bought Monk's Farm. Four, that five of them had come to Hallows End Church that Sunday night. Five, and most speculative of all, that Puckett had suggested that it might be their car that had passed his cottage twice in the night hours of Saturday to Sunday. Now he meant to meet this mysterious family.

He soon found it was going to be no easy matter. Their large farm lay near a by-road as narrow as Church Lane, and the house, a rambling old building built onto in various styles during its three centuries of life, stood quite alone, more than five hundred yards from the present farm buildings. He was able to drive up to it by muddy and rutted tracks, but when he pulled the bell chain of the front door and heard a weary tinkling somewhere deep in the house, he felt that he might be the first stranger to do so for many years.

A rather handsome young woman, with dark gypsyish features, opened the door eighteen inches and said "Yes?"

"May I see Mr. Hickmansworth?

"Who shall I say?"

Carolus gave his name, and was left for some minutes with the door shut in his face. Presently the young woman returned.

"He wants to know on what business?" she said tonelessly.

"Please tell him it is personal but very urgent. I don't want to sell him anything, or ask his opinion for a poll."

"I'll see," she said, and again left him outside a closed door.

This time it was opened by a powerful-looking man in his fifties with a hard ruddy face and thick grey hair.

"I'm Hickmansworth. What the devil do you want?"

Carolus gambled.

"I'm investigating the disappearance of Duncan Humby," he said. "I want to know whether a car of yours was out at a late hour the night before last."

It was evident that he had scored a bulls-eye. The farmer looked at him with an angry baffled expression for a moment, then said, as though he were giving an order rather than an invitation, "Come in."

Carolus followed him to a small, fireless, book-lined room.

"Sit down," he said and did so himself, staring meanwhile at Carolus. "How did you know that?" he said at last.

"I didn't," admitted Carolus. "I guessed it."

There was another brief silence.

"Thing is, I didn't know it myself till yesterday morning." Carolus saw that he would hear more without pressing the matter and sat waiting. "Who are you, anyway? Police?"

"No. I was a client of Humby's. I have promised both his wife and partner I would try to trace him."

Hickmansworth considered.

"Have a drink?" he suggested.

Carolus thought his hand trembled slightly as he poured out two stiff measures of Scotch.

"It's no good your coming here," he said. "There's no one in this house knows anything about it. But what you say about the car is right. It was out during Saturday night."

"Who took it?"

"That's what I'd like to know."

"Was it the station wagon you went to church in on Sunday?"

"You're very observant. Yes. The station wagon. We keep it down at the farm. There's only one garage up here and my son-in-law uses that for his car, a new Austin. We keep a pretty careful check on the mileage of the farm car for income tax purposes. My son went to take it out on Sunday morning and saw the petrol was down, so he checked with the mileage shown when he put it in on Saturday afternoon. The car had gone forty-two miles."

"You are certain no one from here had used it?"

"Of course I am. We play bridge every Saturday night and were up till two in the morning. No one left the house after that."

"So you think someone from outside took your car and used it?"

"I don't think. I know. It's too easy. You saw where the farm buildings are? We hear nothing from there."

"What about the ignition key?"

"It's always left in. We all use the old thing at times."

"I believe you're related to the Neasts?"

Hickmansworth chuckled.

"I thought everyone knew that story," he said. "We are. On the wrong side of the blanket."

"And to Grossiter?"

"Well, yes. But he would never have admitted it. The old man had two older sisters and he quarrelled with both of them. One married Neast and produced those two characters at Monk's Farm. The other was my mother, and she was never married at all because my father's wife was alive and wouldn't divorce him. When eventually she died, my mother and father never bothered to marry. It would have been absurd at their time of life with me grown up as a bastard. Though I daresay if they had, Grossiter might have forgiven them and I might have had a cut at the millions."

Carolus thought he seemed remarkably good-humoured about it all.

"It's good of you to tell me about this," said Carolus.

"I thought everyone knew," he said casually.

"Did you ever meet Grossiter?"

"Never in my life. When the old man quarrelled, he quarrelled. He cut his other sister out, Neasts' mother, for taking my mother's part."

"Did you know he was staying at Monk's Farm?"

Hickmansworth hesitated.

"Yes. I did. Things get about in a district like this."

"But you didn't make any attempt to see him?"

"No. Not while he was staying with those precious cousins of mine. I rather thought I might have a try to see him when he returned home, but it's too late to think of that now. I don't mind telling you this, Deene, but I can't quite see what it has to do with Humby's disappearance."

"Humby, as you must know by now, was taking a will to Grossiter to be signed."

"So you think that one of us may have something to do with Humby? We knew nothing of the man. You'd better stay to lunch and meet my sons. You can ask them some of your questions then. Have another drink?"

"Thanks. The police are exhuming Rudd today," Carolus remarked, watching Hickmansworth.

The man did not turn a hair.

"So I've been told. What are they doing that for? He died in hospital and was buried before Humby ever came to Hallows End."

"They think there's been some interference with the grave," said Carolus steadily.

"Oh, that's it, is it? Perhaps they'll find Humby's corpse in his coffin."

Carolus said nothing for the moment, then changed the subject by remarking that he gathered Hickmansworth did not get on with the Neasts.

"I've known them from childhood. We spent a good deal of our childhood together, as a matter of fact. I put them in the way of buying Monk's Farm when it was on the market. Wonderful little property—I've often wished I'd bought it myself. But I can't stand Holroyd. Never could. Their mother was still alive when I suggested their coming here. So was mine and the two were friends. But Holroyd's no man at all."

"How long have you been here, Mr. Hickmansworth?"

"Best part of thirty years. Father and mother bought this place for me on my twenty-first birthday and moved here themselves from Haysdown where I'd been brought up. About ten years later Holroyd and Cyril bought Monk's Farm. After the two old ladies died, which they did within a year of each other, I told the Neasts to keep away from here and I've never spoken to them since."

"Not even in the last week?"

Hickmansworth seemed amused.

"Clever, aren't you?" he said. "Know everything. I suppose someone saw my old car outside their house. It was my son, as a matter of fact. I wouldn't go near them. But I told him to see if they knew anything about the will."

"And did they?"

"They said not. They had made no enquiries though. They 'didn't like to.'"

"You had some expectations then?"

"Not really. My mother always said there would be nothing. But I couldn't help wondering. After all, I am the man's illegitimate nephew, and he had no one else to leave it to except the Neasts. I didn't fancy their chances. Now come to lunch."

Carolus met Hickmansworth's wife, a dumpy cheerful woman of fifty, and their two sons Edgar and Paul. Edgar was rather good-looking, though his eyes were set too close together, and Paul had a vacant, almost half-witted look. They were both hefty fellows who had been working on the farm all the morning. The son-in-law John Cherry was not at home. He was an estate agent in Cashford and remained there at lunchtime. But his wife, the young woman who had opened the door to Carolus, was present and looked more attractive, Carolus thought.

It was a good meal. There was no sign of any servant in the house, but one of the two women was an excellent cook.

They chattered quite lightly and without embarrassment about events in Hallows End, and Edgar told him again about the mysterious night use of the farm car.

"Was the radiator still warm?" asked Carolus.

"I don't know. I'd had it running a while before I noticed the petrol had gone down."

Hickmansworth himself told them about the exhumation.

"How ghoulish!" said Mrs. Cherry, and nobody else made any comment.

But later, while they were all having coffee, Hickmansworth turned to Carolus.

"Do you think you or the police will ever get at the truth of the whole affair?"

"Oh, yes," said Carolus calmly. "More than one person is involved, and in such a case someone nearly always sees that it pays him or her to give Queen's Evidence."

"Yes, I see that," said Hickmansworth.

Carolus asked whether he might see the station wagon in question and Edgar agreed to take him across to the farm. Carolus saw that it was kept in an open-sided barn and that a good track led from the farm to the road. He also noticed the index number.

"Too easy, wasn't it?" said Edgar.

CHAPTER FIFTEEN

CAROLUS DECIDED NOT TO go to the churchyard during the exhumation, but to wait at the Falstaff where Snow had promised to call on his way back to London. It was not until past five that Snow appeared, and when he did so he shook his head.

"Nothing," he said. "Rudd's coffin lid had never been unscrewed. The old boy was lying there quite undisturbed. Mrs. Rudd was delighted to see his watch on him as she had put it. He's being re-interred now with the parson present."

"How did Whiskins behave over it all?"

"Very excited at first. Said whatever the law, we had no *right* to dig up a dead man. I thought he would get violent at one point. But he calmed down when he saw we meant business. This doesn't get us much farther, does it, Mr. Deene?"

"I don't know. We've eliminated one possibility."

"At a good deal of public expense. You don't have to think of that, Mr. Deene, but I do. It will not do my reputation any good that I asked for an exhumation order that turned out to be for nothing."

Carolus felt that Snow was delicately suggesting the contempt, shared by most CID men, for amateurs, and perhaps wishing he had never come to Carolus at all. As though to reassure him, he gave Snow a piece of information he had gathered.

"Quite by chance," he began diffidently, "I've lighted on a piece of information which may be useful to you."

He then told him Hickmansworth's story about his farm car being used in the night, taking care to show an open mind as to whether or not Hickmansworth and his son were speaking the truth.

"So I suppose you want me to arrest young Hickmansworth and charge him with attempted grave robbery?"

"No, but I wondered if you'd think it worthwhile to run over the car for fingerprints," replied Carolus. "I know how evanescent they are, but on cars you sometimes get a greasy one that's there for months."

Snow, still a little huffy, spoke as though he would be doing Carolus a personal favour by examining the Hickmansworths' farm car.

"I suppose we *could*. But we seem to be catching at straws, Mr. Deene. Give me a nice straightforward case with a bit of laboratory research and only one suspect . . ."

"And only one murder," put in Carolus seriously.

Snow blinked, but said nothing, then stood up to go.

"All right," he conceded. "I'll have the car examined. But I don't see it will tell us much, even if we do find some unexpected prints. What I want to find is Humby."

With this last keep-your-nose-to-the-grindstone suggestion, Snow pulled on his overcoat and prepared to leave. He relented somewhat, however, before leaving Carolus.

"Tell me honestly, Mr. Deene, do you think we're going to clear up this case?"

"To our own satisfaction, yes," said Carolus. "But I doubt if you will ever get a murderer arrested, convicted and hanged. Unless . . ."

"Unless what?"

"Unless somebody elects to give Queen's Evidence."

"There's always that. But at the Yard, we consider a CID man who falls back on it to be in the last infirmity of noble minds."

"Still, there have been plenty of cases where it was necessary, where it was the *only* method of establishing the truth. This may turn out to be one of them."

"Let's hope not, anyway."

Carolus found himself left to the mercy of Mr. Sporter. Before the landlord could ask him how they had got on disinterment-wise, he asked permission to telephone and got through to Thripp.

"I promised to let you know any major developments," he said. "I'm afraid we've drawn another blank. The police got an exhumation order for a man buried here, and executed it this afternoon. It yielded nothing."

"I'm beginning to doubt whether any such researches will. I fear Duncan is lost to us for good. However, I have something to communicate to you which seems to me of the first importance. I decided today that in the circumstances I should be justified in examining the contents of Duncan's private safe. I did so and among other things that surprised me, I found an earlier will of Grossiter."

"Yes. That is important. When was it made?"

"About seven years ago. The fact that Duncan never mentioned it to me suggests that Grossiter exacted his promise of particular secrecy, even from his partner. I see that Duncan typed it on the small machine he keeps at home. I doubt if *any*one knows of it."

"And what were its provisions?"

"What *are* its provisions you may ask, for this is the will which can now be proved. It is a perfectly legal document. Its provisions are very simple. His estate was to be divided into four equal parts, one of which was to go to each of three branches of his family and the fourth to Darkin."

"What branches?"

"They are named as: One, the Neasts, Holroyd and Cyril; Two, Hickmansworth, Gerald; Three, Grossiter, Raymond; Four, Darkin, Simon George. Since Grossiter's son Raymond is dead and left no issue, the sum for each of the remaining beneficiaries will be a considerable one. Although none of them was mentioned in the will Duncan had drawn—but which was never signed—I see no means of disputing this one."

"I see."

"Is this information likely to hasten your investigation at all, Deene? Every day of this is agony for Theodora, not to mention my own anxiety."

"It is certainly very valuable," said Carolus.

After he hung up, he stood staring for some moments at the notes he had made, then picked up the local telephone guide. He found the Neasts' number.

Holroyd answered.

"This is Carolus Deene. I should like to speak to Mr. Darkin, please."

Another man might have repeated "Deene? Darkin?" incredulously, but Holroyd only paused a moment before saying quite civilly, "Certainly. Hold on a moment, will you?"

Darkin, when he answered, was another matter. He sounded anxious and spoke in a low voice as though he did not want to be heard by those near him.

"Yes, Mr. Deene?"

"Let me be the first to congratulate you," said Carolus cheerfully. "An earlier will of Mr. Grossiter's has come to light by which you benefit."

There was no cry of joy from the other end, or anything like it.

"I don't quite understand," said Darkin.

"As you know, Mr. Humby had been instructed by your late employer to draw up a will. It was generally believed, and

Mr. Humby's partner shared that belief, that Grossiter had intended till then to die intestate. But in going through the papers
in Humby's private safe he has found another, perfectly legal
will of Grossiter's, signed and witnessed some seven years ago,
by which you benefit."

"Oh . . ."

"I should like to see you alone, Darkin. I can give you the
details of this."

"I don't know . . ."

"I am staying at the Falstaff Hotel for the night. Could you
come up here?"

A struggle seemed to be going on at the other end.

"Yes. I'll come," said Darkin at last.

"It would perhaps be as well if you said nothing about this
for the moment."

"I understand."

Darkin said no more and, without even specifying a time,
closed the conversation.

An hour later, when Carolus was taking a breath of fresh
air and a brief respite from the conversation of Mr. Sporter, he
saw the Rolls Royce, with Darkin driving it, turn into the car
park. The man came lumbering towards him with his bear-like
walk on large splayed feet.

They greeted each other briefly and Carolus led Darkin to a
small room near the bar, unfortunately known as the Snuggery.
No one else was there.

Carolus had no intention of letting the initiative pass out of
his hands. He knew that Darkin was agog to learn something
of the sum that he might receive, so he was determined to ask
his questions before discussing that.

"Had you any idea that such a will existed?"

"I could scarcely believe that Mr. Grossiter would neglect
me entirely. But as I told you I am not a man to pay much

attention to such things. Mr. Grossiter and I were, I venture to say, friends."

"Then why was he leaving you out of the new will? I have seen a draft of this and there is no question about it."

"I cannot say and I should not wish to speculate. But might it not have been his intention to save death duties by making a monetary gift?"

"I hardly think so. He was doing that for young Spaull and no mention was made of you."

"Spaull," said Darkin with narrowed eyes, then seemed to remember himself. "That was very proper. The young man was his natural grandson."

"Oh. You knew that? Most people thought Spaull was his son."

"Mr. Grossiter gave me the facts when he instructed me never to allow the man into his presence."

There was a long silence broken by Darkin with a startling question.

"Do you believe I killed Humby, Mr. Deene?"

"No," said Carolus at once. "I don't believe anything of the sort. But I do believe you know a good deal more than you've said."

Darkin eyed him sombrely.

"Don't *you*, Mr. Deene? Know a good deal more than you've said?"

"Yes," returned Carolus. "I do."

"For instance, you know about this will that's been found, and by which you say I benefit."

"Yes," said Carolus. "I know about that. And you know interesting things, like what time the Neasts came home that Monday afternoon, and *whether anyone was with them*. You know a good deal of what happened that night. Shall we exchange information?"

"I think I have told you all I know, Mr. Deene. If you don't wish to inform me about Mr. Grossiter's will, I must wait till I am told by the solicitors."

"Do you know Hickmansworth by sight?" asked Carolus suddenly.

"No. I do not."

"Or any of his family?"

"No."

"But you know the Rector here, Mr. Whiskins?"

"Yes."

"And you know Lionel Thripp, Humby's partner?"

"Yes."

"And Mrs. Caplan, the Humbys' housekeeper?"

"I have seen the lady."

"And would recognise her?"

"Yes.

"You are very observant and you remember faces. Yet you say that you don't know any of the Hickmansworths?"

"To the best of my knowledge, no. A young man came to see Mr. Holroyd Neast one afternoon; I caught a glimpse of him as he got into his car. It might have been one of Hickmansworth's sons. Holroyd did not enlighten me."

Carolus eyed the man keenly.

"Do you know where Duncan Humby is now?" he asked. "He or his corpse?"

"No, Mr. Deene, I do not. I have not the slightest idea."

For some reason Carolus believed this.

"Now let me ask you something, Mr. Deene. Do you think that you will find Humby?"

"Yes."

"And the truth about this whole affair?"

"Certainly. I have not the slightest doubt of obtaining a conviction."

Darkin quavered a little as he asked, "What for?"

"Murder," said Carolus coolly.

"Oh, so you believe there has been a murder."

"There has been at least one already."

"*Already?*"

"Yes. I should not be surprised to hear of another. When some wild beasts are cornered they become very, very dangerous."

Darkin said nothing for a moment, then, speaking almost in a whisper he asked, "How can you be so sure? Of learning the truth, I mean?"

"I'll tell you. In this case, whatever this case is, whether of murder, kidnapping or manslaughter, more than one person is involved in the crime. When that happens, and the case is hopeless for the criminals, one of them always has the intelligence to offer Queen's Evidence. That will happen here."

Darkin's large hands clasped and unclasped.

"I see what you mean. But what makes you think that the case is hopeless, as you put it?"

"I'll tell you. I know a little too much, Darkin. I can't yet prove it, but that's only a matter of time. I know who was in Humby's car that afternoon and what happened to him. I know why Rudd's grave was interfered with and by whom. I even know, or have a shrewd idea, who cracked Spaull over the head last Saturday night. And I know a bit more than is comfortable for them about several people whose names have been connected with this case. So I know that the case is hopeless for those who are guilty."

Darkin seemed to pull himself together.

"Well, that's very nice for you, Mr. Deene. You must be a very clever man. You seem to know a great deal about this case of a missing man. The only thing I notice about it is, that what you *don't* know is where that missing man may be. If anyone has done anything to cause him to be missing, as it were, I shouldn't think that person's case was 'hopeless', as you say, until that missing man is found."

"But then it would be too late, surely. The police don't want Queen's Evidence from someone they can hang for murder anyway."

Another silence.

"Besides," went on Carolus, "the police don't want Queen's Evidence from two people. Our hypothetical friend might find he had been anticipated, in which case his Queen's Evidence would become simply a confession of his crime."

"Very interesting, Mr. Deene. But I don't find it altogether convincing "

"You will, Darkin, you will. Now, would you like me to tell you about Grossiter's will?"

Darkin waited.

"I've no figures, mind you, and I'm not a lawyer. But I gather that after death duties are paid, you will receive a third of the whole property. It should be a very large sum."

"Yes. You say this will was made seven years ago?"

"About that."

"Do you know who witnessed it?"

"Yes. Someone named Edith Cupper."

"That's a woman who worked for Mr. Grossiter. She had only just started then or she might have been remembered."

"She was later. Fifteen thousand pounds was to go to her at the same time as the ten thousand to Spaull."

"I see."

"What makes the discovery of this early will so interesting is to think what would have been lost to whom if the second will had ever been signed. You, the Neasts and Hickmansworth would have lost everything that will now come to you."

"Mrs. Cupper won't lose, because I shall make it up to her. But I don't know anything about the man Spaull."

"No. I don't see that you could be expected to. How does it feel to be a rich man, Darkin?"

"One thing you seem to forget or deliberately to ignore, Mr. Deene, was that I worked for seventeen years for Mr. Grossiter, putting up with all his fads and tempers. I was devoted to him. I do not think that whatever benefit may come to me will be ill-deserved."

"Yet Grossiter himself seems to have thought otherwise."

"He was a very strange man. Headstrong yet easily influenced. Someone who saw him during those last few days before he sent for Humby might have caused him to change his mind."

Carolus looked at him closely.

"You think that? Someone like Spaull, for instance?"

"Yes. Someone like Spaull."

"But that would scarcely account for the withdrawal of everything from the Neasts and Hickmansworth."

"I never knew, and I doubt if anyone else did, that Mr. Grossiter recognised the existence of Hickmansworth. I never heard the name till we came down here. As for the Neasts, I'm afraid Mr. Grossiter was not very comfortable at Monk's Farm. He intended to leave that week. He said he had come for ten days and should stay for ten days, but he kept to his room most of the time. He disapproved of Cyril Neast's drinking and felt a personal dislike for Holroyd Neast. He thought the house was disgracefully dirty and that he was neglected. There was open trouble between him and Holroyd more than once."

"I see."

"Thank you for giving me this information, Mr. Deene," said Darkin rising. "I suppose I shall hear officially quite soon."

Carolus left the Snuggery, followed by Darkin who accompanied him to the saloon bar. As soon as they entered they became aware of the Neast brothers standing at the far corner of the bar, looking sullen and out of place. Carolus and Darkin crossed to them. The brothers greeted them without enthusiasm, though Holroyd wore his smile.

"I have been congratulating Darkin," Carolus said. "Your uncle made a will seven years ago which has just been discovered in his own safe. By it Darkin receives a third of your uncle's property."

"And the other two thirds?"

"One of them is to be divided between you two."

"And the other?"

"The other goes to Hickmansworth," said Carolus, and, before he could hear any comment, walked away.

Chapter Sixteen

Next morning when Snow dropped in, Carolus told him he was returning to Newminster.

"There's nothing more for me to do here."

"You think you know the truth about all this?"

"Yes, but I haven't a hope of even convincing you, let alone proving it. I haven't even much circumstantial evidence. In other words, I've got only an amateur's theory without support or substance. I should be ashamed to put it to you or anyone else. A couple of whys would demolish it."

"And you don't think you can substantiate it by continuing to work with us?"

"No. Unless there are some new developments."

"Such as?"

"Such as another death. Or the discovery of Humby's body—for I believe him to be dead."

"You don't even want to see the result of the fingerprint test on Hickmansworth's station wagon?"

"I think I know what that will be. But I don't think it will help us much, unless we come to know where the car was driven that night. I'd be grateful if you'd phone me in an idle moment . . ."

"Thanks. I haven't many of those. Still, I'll phone you the result of that test. It was, after all, you who suggested it. I think you're a bit of a defeatist, Mr. Deene."

"Perhaps. You'll find I'm interested enough if anything breaks. It's just that until that happens I'm wasting time."

"To go away and wait for another murder . . ."

"I didn't suggest that. We don't know there has been one murder yet. I don't think there will be another death. Unless, of course, we're dealing with a lunatic or lunatics, and so far there's no sign of that."

"None at all," agreed Snow.

"Besides, you know, I have my job to think of. The school terms starts on Friday. And I don't really think you'll be sorry to have me out of the way."

Before Carolus left the Falstaff, he had a word with Mr. Sporter.

"This is my telephone number in Newminster," he said. "If anything startling happens down here, will you let me know?"

"I'll be only too glad, natch, to do so. Even if it only seems triv to me," said the landlord. "Guest-wise you've been exemp."

"Thanks," said Carolus and was soon on his way to Newminster, perhaps, he thought, for the last time over this road.

Mrs. Stick received him sceptically.

"That's what you *say*, sir, that you've finished with it. Me and Stick knows better. It only needs one of them to come calling here and you'll be off again."

"But school starts on Friday, Mrs. Stick."

"School! A lot you care about school when you're after one of these murderers. I don't know how the Headmaster puts up with it, upon my word I don't. I was only saying to Stick, whatever do the boys' parents think, I said, having their sons taught by someone who's larking about with murderers half his time."

"What have we for lunch, Mrs. Stick?" asked Carolus, to lead her to happier topics. But she was curt.

"Potto fur," she snapped and went out to her kitchen.

Carolus spent the day working on his notes—not of the Hallows End case, but of constitutional changes under Cromwell and the Commonwealth, for the Lower Sixth. It was not until six o'clock that Mrs. Stick came to summon him to the telephone.

"What did I tell you?" she asked triumphantly. "It's one of your policemen. Snow, he calls himself."

"Why not?" asked Carolus mildly. "That's his name. He has been here before."

Snow sounded pleased.

"We found a small collection of good prints," he said. "They were all pretty close together—apart from those of the Hickmansworths, of course. Whose do you think?"

"Cyril Neast's," said Carolus.

"If you know so much, Mr. Deene, I don't know why you've chucked up the case. Cyril Neast has a perfectly good explanation for them, however. When young Hickmansworth came to Monk's Farm to ask if they knew anything about the will, Cyril came out into the road with him to see him off. He stood talking with him for some minutes after Edgar Hickmansworth was in the driving seat. He was leaning on the car. Young Hickmansworth remembers him being there."

"Where were the prints?"

"On the bonnet, as a matter of fact. He must have opened the bonnet to flood the carburettor or something. Edgar doesn't remember him doing that."

"Well, thanks," said Carolus.

"As I said, it doesn't get us much farther."

But it seemed to make Carolus very thoughtful for the rest of that evening. As Mrs. Stick reported to her husband, he sat in his chair without a book, "looking nowhere, as you might say. You could tell he was thinking of murders."

Next morning, Wednesday, he was undisturbed until a little past eleven when Sporter rang up. The landlord of the Falstaff sounded very unlike himself. He was serious, somewhat awed, it would seem, by the solemnity of his news.

"Darkin's dead," he stated. "Apparently suicide. He was found in a meadow near Monk's Farm with a twelve-bore beside him and most of his head shot away."

Carolus cut him off as briefly as he politely could.

"I'll come straightaway," he said, and with only a brief word to Mrs. Stick, he started out on the familiar road to Hallows End.

He had lost all hesitation. He no longer thought of awaiting the discovery of Humby or anything else. He recognised that he must act quickly if yet another life was not to be lost.

He found Snow at Monk's Farm. Snow also had a set face and spoke curtly. He did not remind Carolus that he had said he didn't think there would be another death unless they were dealing with lunatics.

"You'd better see Stonegate if you want details. He found the body. Only one thing I can tell you that may be relevant: Darkin phoned a solicitor yesterday, John Stuffart of Stuffart and Stuffart in Cashford, and made an appointment for today. Otherwise it's all yours. Death instantaneous of course. Barrel probably in his mouth. Half his head blown away. There'll be a post mortem."

"You might examine the guts as well."

Snow gave a grim smile.

"If you'd seen the thing, you wouldn't bother about poison."

"I think I should. I can only suggest it, of course, but I'd like very much to see a report on the contents of the stomach and ducts."

"I shall get that automatically. A post mortem covers everything. If it's at all unusual I'll let you know. Now I must get back to the grindstone. I can't afford fancy theorising, Mr. Deene."

Carolus grinned.

"Where's Stonegate?" he asked.

"He has taken the day off in anticipation of the rush to see him. If he wasn't the last to see Darkin alive, he was at least the first to see him dead. It's a big day for him. You'll find him at his cottage or at one of the pubs."

"Thanks. One other small thing. Any footprints near the body?"

"None found. But the place might have been chosen. Short hard grass. Not a chance of a footprint or anything else."

Carolus drove straight to Stonegate's thatched cottage. The door was opened by Doll almost before he knocked. She did not seem to find the occasion a solemn one.

"You can't help laughing at Dad," she said. "He's sitting there in his best suit waiting for the photographers. He said to me just now, he said, 'I think I'll give the name as George Stonegate instead of Joel. It'll look better in the papers. Less old-fashioned'."

A stern voice from the inner room called Doll to her duties, and she showed Carolus in.

"Ah, yes," said Stonegate. "The gentleman from Newminster interested in crime. Well, you've got enough of it now to keep you busy."

"How did you come to find the remains of Darkin, Stonegate?"

"You may well say remains. If you could have seen it. With the ground all round spattered too . . ."

"Yes. How did you chance to come on it?"

"It wasn't chance. I was carrying out my duties. Mr. Neast wanted that hedge repaired."

"Which hedge?"

"The hedge between our land and Hickmansworths'. It's fallen in in places. You used not to be able to get through that hedge wherever you looked. But in this last year or two it's gone all to pieces. So I was on my way down there to see what it needed. I took the old path which used to lead right from Monk's Farm to Hickmansworths' in the old days. But when they fell out Neasts had the stile taken away and the hedge closed. Only you could still get through there. The Rector had something to say at the time about it being a Right of Way. Anyway, I took that path. Just as I was coming to the boundary between the two farms what should I see but . . ."

"Darkin," supplied Carolus.

"Yes. What there was left of him. You could see ten feet away where there were bits of brain and that. It would turn you up. I used to work in a slaughter-house and . . ."

"Yes. How was he lying?"

"On his back. You could see that by his jacket, not by his face. There was nothing much left of that. It was like . . ."

"Where was the gun?"

"Right beside him and his thumb still caught round the trigger. He'd probably leaned down over the gun with its barrel in his mouth and pulled, so it had knocked him right back. You've never seen such a sight in your life. All over the grass . . ."

"What time was this?"

"When I found him? Must have been getting on for ten o'clock. I'd been up since seven, but over the other side beyond the church."

"Did you hear the shot?"

"I thought you'd ask me that. They all will, you can be sure. Well," he announced magnanimously, "I'm not going to say I did because I didn't. Isn't it enough to have found his remains as you call them? It wasn't pleasant, I can tell you that. Why, before I knew, I'd stepped in it and all my boot . . ."

"Surely if the shot had been fired since you reached the farm, you'd have heard it?"

"Well, I'm not going to say I did because I didn't," repeated Stonegate. "But it's hard to see why not. I was out working earlier than usual—before half past seven, and you wouldn't think he'd of got up and gone out after rabbits before then, would you? I mean it wouldn't have been hardly light."

"Do you know if anyone else heard the shot?"

Stonegate looked cagey.

"I've been given to understand," he said grandly, "that Mrs. Rudd has some story to that effect, but you know how much you can believe women. I'd say I'd heard it if I had . . ."

"You bet you would," said Doll, coming into the room. "He can't get over it," she explained to Carolus, "it being Mrs. Rudd and not him heard the poor man shoot himself. 'Another time', he says, 'if ever you hear anything like shots and that, you let me know'. He's a scream really."

"But you're sure you would have heard it, Stonegate, if it had been fired after you reached the farm?"

"Certainly I should. That's what I say. He can't have done it any later than seven-fifteen say, or I should have heard him. Hullo! Who's this coming? Doll. Tell him Mr. Stonegate's engaged for the minute but will see him in due course. It's a reporter, you can see that. Has he got his camera, Doll? And you don't show him in till I'm ready. Where's my boot with the blood on it?"

Carolus made his escape and drove to Mrs. Rudd's where he received rather a different welcome.

"Oh, it's you again is it?" the big woman said. "You'd better come in out of the cold. It's a nasty chilly day."

"I understand you heard a shot fired early this morning?" said Carolus.

"Yes. I told the police gentlemen all about it."

"What time was it?"

"I can't say, not to the minute. I was worrying about Mr. Spaull going off without his breakfast."

"Mr. Spaull? I thought he'd gone back to his work in Newminster?"

"So he had. But he came down last night on his motorbike to get his washing he'd left behind because I hadn't finished it for him. It was such a nasty night, I said, why don't you stay till the morning, because his room was just as he left it and it wasn't a night to go running about on a motorbike. So he said he would, but he'd have to be off early in the morning to get to his work in time but he wouldn't disturb me going off. Whatever time it was I don't know, but I heard him getting dressed and then creeping downstairs not to wake me."

"Did you hear him start his motorbike?"

"No. He must have wheeled it away not to make a noise round here, but he was like that, thinking of others instead of himself all the time. After he'd gone I couldn't get to sleep again thinking I might have got up and given him a bit of breakfast, when suddenly I heard this shot."

"How long after Spaull left the cottage?"

"It's hard to say, but it must have been at least half an hour I should think. You couldn't tell where it came from, but it wasn't near at hand. It might have been from where they found the body. When I heard about it I said to myself that must have been the shot, I said. It's not nice to think of though, is it? I mean I wasn't much taken with that Darkin but you don't want anyone to shoot themselves."

As Carolus left the cottage he saw Holroyd Neast standing by his car.

"Good morning," said Neast, almost ingratiatingly. "This is a bad business, isn't it?"

"Yes," said Carolus. "Was there nothing in his behaviour which might have led you to fear something of this kind?"

"Absolutely nothing. On the contrary, he seemed very cheerful yesterday. He had arranged to see a solicitor about his inheritance today."

"How did you know that, Mr. Neast?"

Holroyd's smile seemed broader and more mirthless than ever.

"He told us. In fact he asked if we could recommend a good solicitor for the purpose. Our own man is Drury of Lycett Dobbs in Cashford, but I knew of Stuffart as a very sound chap. So Darkin rang him up straightaway and made an appointment for this morning. There was a large sum of money involved."

"Wasn't it very unusual for Darkin to go out with a gun?"

"Not at all. He liked having a pot at the rabbits in that meadow where his body was found. He had borrowed my gun and been there several times before."

"Did he have any luck?"

"Luck?"

"With rabbits, I mean?"

"Yes. He brought home a brace only last Sunday."

"He always went in the early morning?"

"Yes. It's the best time. He always went at the same time, too, until today when he went earlier. Always left the house at a quarter to eight. My brother and I used to pull his leg about it and ask whom he was meeting in the Long Meadow."

"Did he sleep well, Mr. Neast?"

"Sleep well? I couldn't say, really. He did say once that he always took a mild sedative at night. But plenty of people do that. He got up early, if that's any test."

"What were his plans?"

"I don't think he had made any. Until he knew about the money I think he intended to find a similar job. But he was very shaken by my uncle's death and we made him welcome so far as we could until he had decided. Naturally when he heard he would be a rich man, it changed everything."

"Naturally. Thank you for your information, Mr. Neast. You must be tired of being the centre of such a storm."

"We should like to see it cleared up, of course. But I have learned to take life as it comes."

That evening Snow and Carolus met again at the Falstaff

"I've just got the results of the post mortem through," said Snow. "They did a rush job for us because the circumstances justified it. You were quite right. They found enough poison in the man to kill two people."

"What poison?"

"Quite an ordinary thing called Thelodocticylin. It is used in small quantities in the making of certain tranquillising pills."

"So Darkin was dead before the shot was fired into his mouth?"

"Not necessarily. An almost empty bottle of Somnifax tablets, the tranquillisers made from Thelodocticylin, was found in his pocket. The quantity found in Darkin would not have had an instantaneous effect. Like many suicides he could have had fears about the effectiveness of poison. He may have been murdered, as you suggest, but on the other hand there is nothing final to prove that he did not take poison, then shoot himself for double security."

"I see. This thing's getting out of hand, isn't it?"

"Let me say frankly, Mr. Deene, that although I would be reprimanded severely for saying such a thing to a private investigator, I tell you that any help you can give me at this point would make me really grateful."

"There is just one thing I can try," said Carolus. "It's a long shot and may come to nothing. But it's all I can suggest."

"What is it?"

"I'm going tomorrow to Haysdown."

Snow stared at him as though he were insane.

"Where and what is Haysdown?" he asked loudly.

"It's a village about eighteen miles from here. Hickmansworth was brought up there. I should like to know a little more about Hickmansworth."

Snow seemed about to explode, but said no more. He evidently thought that Carolus was being facetious.

CHAPTER SEVENTEEN

IT WAS A CLEAR WINDY morning when Carolus set out for Haysdown, and, he scarcely had time to reflect, the last day of the school holidays. This journey, as he had told Snow, was a long shot, longer than he would admit to himself, yet if it yielded what he obstinately tried to hope it would, the case would be wide open and tidily finished before he began teaching.

He found the village, though in the same fold of the hills as Hallows End, to be entirely different from it in appearance. Where Hallows End was huddled among trees, damp-looking and in most of its buildings ancient, Haysdown was spread out over a hillside with more bright new bungalows and building estates than old cottages or houses.

The inn, however, was old and he made straight for it, reflecting that throughout his career as an investigator he had gained more information over bars than in all the private houses he had entered. He was no sentimentalist about pubs and disliked the artily restored and picturesque ones, but where else, in any village or suburb, could a man start his enquiries, whether he was looking for a house to let, a char to employ, or a murderer to convict? The Duke of Clarence, with its square Victorian front and geranium-filled window boxes, promised to be no exception.

It had been open only about ten minutes when Carolus entered the bar. This was one of those large rooms, used almost universally, that are sometimes found in the smarter country pubs. Carolus guessed there was a small saloon full of polished brass used by a few couples on Saturday night, but that the business of the house was carried on here. His only fellow customer was a very old man who, with the shyness of one from another epoch, would not look up at him or answer his "Good morning."

The landlord, a stoutish man in his fifties, was busy polishing glasses. Carolus ordered his usual Scotch and soda and respectfully observed the general silence for a few minutes.

Presently he felt he might venture on a crab-like approach to subjects he wanted to introduce.

"Windy this morning," he said.

The landlord, who kept a pipe in his mouth, held a glass up to the light.

"It *is* windy," he agreed.

"I suppose you get it pretty strong here. You're open to it."

"Yes, we *do* get it strong," the landlord cheerfully concurred, and added, "especially when it's round the North East."

"Been here long?" dared Carolus.

"Born here," said the landlord. "Father had the pub before me, and his before that. This is one of the few houses in England that's been in one family for three generations."

"Interesting," said Carolus, and recognising at least a temporary check, was silent again.

When he returned to the attack, he came in from a different quarter.

"I've just come from Hallows End," he observed. "It's in a bit of a turmoil, as you can imagine."

"I'm not at all surprised," said the landlord. "They must be wondering who it'll be next."

Carolus had to retreat.

"That's about it," he agreed and there was yet another pause. This time he attacked head on.

"Did you ever know some people called Hickmansworth?" he asked.

"Well, of course I did," said the landlord rather scornfully. "They had what we call the manor, though it's no bigger than several other large houses. Young Gerry was just about my age."

Recognising in "young Gerry" the grey-haired Hickmansworth of today, Carolus did no more than nod. With any luck he had set the machine of memory working and wouldn't have to ask another question.

"He was a lad," said the landlord reflectively.

"I can well believe it."

"Up to anything, you might say."

"Yes."

"Full of devilment. They couldn't do anything with him."

"I'll have another Scotch, and what will you have?" encouraged Carolus.

"Thank you. I'll have a bitter. Yes, young Gerry was a boy."

Reminiscence would break out at any minute, Carolus knew.

"All sorts of larks he got up to."

"Mm?"

"I remember once . . . but it wouldn't do to tell you about that because the girl's married now and got grown-up children."

"No. Perhaps not."

"Another time he caught a couple of big rats and shut them up in the pulpit which was one of those with doors to them. You should have seen what happened when the vicar in those days, a little nervous chap called Meiklejohn, went up to preach his sermon."

"I can imagine it," Carolus assured the landlord.

"Then there was the time he had a fight with a lad a little bigger than himself and got him down on the ground and tried

to strangle him. They say he would have done if two men hadn't
come along and pulled him off. This other lad couldn't speak
for a week and hasn't got over it to this day. Yes, he was a
proper little demon, that Gerry Hickmansworth."

"Sounds like it," agreed Carolus.

"I never took to his cousins, though. They used to come
down and stay with him. Name of Neast. They were just the
opposite to what young Gerry was. You'd say butter wouldn't
melt in their mouths. They'd give him away, too, or let him take
the blame for anything they'd had a hand in."

"Did they spend much time here?"

"Most of the summer they were here every year. But I never
took to them. This Gerry used to lead like a gang of us young-
sters, and I was what he called his lieutenant. It was all right till
these Neasts came along, then you never knew. I'd found the
headquarters for us and I never wanted Gerry to tell them where
it was because I knew they'd give it away, but he told them in
the end. It was a dead secret, too. You know what boys are."

"Where was it?"

The landlord smiled.

"It's funny," he said, "but even now I don't like saying where
it is, not after all these years. It was what they call a Dane-hole
out in the wood."

"A Dane-hole? Here?" asked Carolus, the history master in
him almost as interested as the detective.

"That's what they used to say. But another man who knew
a lot about all that said it was an old mine shaft. I'll tell you
what it was like. You couldn't hardly see the entrance because it
was all grown over, but when you found it, you went stooping
down a long tunnel which sloped downwards, till you came to
like a big cave. You could tell it had been dug out by men ever
so many years ago. Those that called it a Dane-hole said it was
where all the people from the village used to hide when the

Danish invaders were coming, and those who thought it was a mine said that's how the Romans made mines when they had no means of getting people up and down a vertical shaft. Anyhow, that's where our little gang used to hold its meetings. You see, I heard of it from my father, who used to play there as a boy. It was like a secret passed on between the boys of each generation."

"Very, very interesting," said Carolus. "I should like to see it."

"I don't know whether I could find the entrance now after all these years," said the landlord.

"I expect you could. Somehow one doesn't forget things like that from childhood."

"You interested in archy . . . archo . . ."

"Archaeology? Yes. I am."

"Tell you what then, we'll go out there this afternoon and see if I can find it for you."

"Splendid. That's very kind of you."

"I know how to get there, mind you. You stop at Crabling's cottage on the Scorton road and turn into the woods from there. But how you pace it out I've forgotten. Still, we'll see."

Carolus saw no movement and heard no sound from the old gentleman in the bar, but there must have been some communication, telepathic perhaps, between him and the landlord. For the landlord at this moment said, "Ready for your other pint then, Mr. Gosforth?" He fetched the glass tankard from the table and filled it.

"What time do you close?" asked Carolus.

"Two o'clock. I'll be ready soon after."

Carolus ate a cold lunch by the bar fire, then drove at the landlord's instructions by a wood-surrounded road for a distance of half a mile.

"There's the cottage," said the landlord. "Stop in front of that."

As he got out of the car, Carolus became aware of a frowning female face at the window of the cottage.

"That's Mrs. Crabling," said the landlord. "She's a proper old bitch. Gives her husband the hell of a life. He's a nice chap who likes a pint now and again and the look of a pretty girl. But not if she knows it! She's so prim and narrow-minded . . . well, dirty-minded some would say, that she won't let him out of her sight if she can help it and thinks every girl in the village is no better than she should be and after him. She tried to have the dances stopped in the village hall because she said they led to immorality afterwards. Now what we've got to find is this Dane-hole."

The landlord led the way through a gap in the hedge into the autumn-scented wood. They rustled deep drifts of brown leaves as they walked and the damp beautiful smell of these, and the lichen-covered trees, and the mossy trunks of elms had a nostalgic air, so that Carolus remembered his own boyhood adventures in such woods as these.

"It's not more than twenty yards from the road if I remember right," said the landlord, looking about him. "But just how did we used to come? You stay here a minute to mark the direction and I'll see if I can pick up the track."

Carolus did as he was told and the landlord disappeared, rooting about in the stillness of the woods like some great animal. Minutes began to pass but Carolus waited patiently, knowing that there was nothing he could do. He was rewarded at last by a shout from over on his left.

He found the landlord by a rough cavity.

"Looks as though someone's been here lately," the landlord said and pointed to the broken undergrowth and branches.

"It does."

From that moment the fear, or the hope, or the wild suspicion of what he would find in the Dane-hole became certainty. The landlord pulled out an electric torch he had brought along, and they began their slow stooping way down the long tunnel. It was a painful experience, for it was impossible to stand upright and the shaft or passage continued for nearly twenty yards.

At the end of it was a round chamber some twenty-two feet in diameter and ten foot high. Over against the far wall, lying in several inches of muddy water, was the fully clothed body of a man. Carolus had to turn it over before he recognised Duncan Humby. The face was horribly scarred and discoloured and he judged the man to be at least a week dead.

The landlord, not surprisingly, lost his head a little.

"Let's get out of here," he whispered fervently. Then louder — "Come on. Let's get OUT!"

Carolus laid a handkerchief over the face and followed the landlord as he trundled through the passage towards the light.

"What are you going to do?" he asked Carolus when they stood in the wood free of that dank ancient world they had visited.

"Phone the police,' said Carolus, making for the car.

"Where? Over at Cashford?"

"No. The CID man on the Hallows End case. That was the body of Duncan Humby, the missing solicitor."

The landlord looked at him with sudden suspicion.

"Did you know it was there?" he asked.

"I didn't *know*. But when you began to tell me about the place and the boys who played there, I thought there might be a chance of finding it."

They reached the Duke of Clarence and Carolus got through, by great good fortune, to Snow, who was working in the office that day waiting results of certain tests. He told him his news.

Snow took it calmly.

"Will you wait there?" he asked. "I'll be down with a team within three hours. It's three-fifteen now so I shall hope to make it by six. Where shall I come?"

"To the local pub, the Duke of Clarence. The landlord knows where to take you if I'm not there."

"Not there?"

"I have something else to do here in Haysdown. I expect I shall have finished it by then, though."

As he put the receiver down he saw that the landlord, who was visibly shaken, had poured out two whiskies.

"No, thanks," said Carolus. "Too early for me. You have those two on me. I'd rather have some tea. Then I have to go out and call on those people with the cottage opposite."

"The Crablings? I wish you luck. You won't get far with her. I doubt if she'll let you in the cottage."

But he was wrong. Mrs. Crabling was a forbidding-looking woman with a pinched and angry face who opened her door a few inches and said, "Yes?" very sharply.

Carolus said, "Good afternoon. May I see your husband, please?"

"What do you want with him? I saw you with that publican this afternoon. If it's to get him to play in his darts team again, he's not well enough."

"No. It's not that."

"He's got a bad cold. That's why he's away from work. Do you come from the quarry?"

"No. But I'd be grateful to you both for a little information."

"Whatever about?"

"Couldn't I come in and explain?"

"Well, I suppose you *could*. Only I don't know you, do I?"

"I'm really quite harmless, Mrs. Crabling."

"So you may be. Who's to know? Very well, come in then. Only mind those dirty boots on my clean carpet. Your coat's all over mud. Wherever have you been? I saw you going into the woods this afternoon. Come on then; he's in here."

Seated by a warm fire, Carolus faced Mrs. Crabling and her big red-faced husband,

"Now what is it?" she asked.

"I have been investigating the case of the lawyer who disappeared over at Hallows End. You may have read about it in the papers?"

"I'm not saying we haven't but . . ."

"This afternoon I found him. Or rather his dead body. In the woods here."

Mrs. Crabling seemed temporarily knocked out. "You don't mean there's a corpse out there?" she asked at last.

"It's well concealed. The police will be here presently to take it away."

"I should think so. Suppose one of us was to have come on it? You can't have corpses left on decent people's doorsteps. It's not right. How did it come to be there? That's what I want to know."

Crabling said nothing, but looked from his wife to Carolus.

"I'm hoping one of you may be able to help me answer that, Mrs. Crabling."

"You're not going to make out we had anything to do with it, are you?"

"No. No. But you may have seen something without realising how important it was. Do many cars stop along this road?"

"No, because I won't have it. After one of the dances in the village, there used to be one or two, but I told the policeman here that if he didn't stop it I would. Disgusting, it was. Young fellows with girls who ought to know better. You never know what they might not get up to, do you?"

"Yes," said Carolus but left the point.

"Has there been one lately?" he asked. "Last Saturday night, for instance?"

The Crablings exchanged glances.

"That was the night," said Mrs. Crabling.

"Yes, that was it," said Crabling, speaking for the first time.

"There was one of these dances in the village," went on Mrs. Crabling. "I'd have them stopped if I had my way. People carrying on in front of everybody like that. It's not right and it's not decent. Dancing, they call it. I'd call it something worse than that."

"What?" asked Carolus curiously.

"Never you mind. Anyway, there was one because I saw the posters about it. I said to my husband, if any of them come out here afterwards with their nasty goings-on I shall report them, I said. Well, wouldn't you?"

"No," said Carolus. "And did any of them?"

"One did. Only it wasn't until you'd have thought they'd all been home by that time that it happened. Just after three o'clock in the morning, it was. Would you believe it? Whatever had they been doing all that time, because the dance is over at twelve?"

"I can't think," said Carolus.

"It came along so sly, too. I happened to be awake or I should never have heard it. It seemed to switch its engine off and just glide to opposite here. I looked out of the window and before I could see anything to speak of, it had turned its lights off."

"Tttt," said Carolus sympathetically.

"I wasn't going to have that. Not that, I wasn't going to have. It's a public danger, let alone anything else. Out there with no lights on. So I woke my husband."

Poor devil, thought Carolus.

"I said we can't have this right outside our front gate, didn't I, Arthur?"

Crabling nodded.

"I said, you go down and tell them to clear off or I'll set the police on them. Why, they might have been doing *any*thing out there at that time. So my husband went down, but when he got there, they'd gone."

"What, the car?"

"No. These two that were in it."

"How did you know there were two?"

"It stands to reason, doesn't it? I've told you what goes on after these dances. So it was really worse than what I'd thought. He'd taken her into the woods. That's how you read about girls being murdered and it serves them right if you ask me."

"So you came back to bed?" Carolus asked Crabling.

"When he told me what had happened, I made up my mind to stop it once and for all. Right outside my house! You'd think people would have more shame. So I said to my husband, you go down and take the number of that car and I shall report it, I said. Which he did, and I've got it wrote on a piece of paper in my bag."

"Did you report it?"

"Well, what with my husband being laid up with a cold next day I never got round to it. But you let them try it again."

"I don't think they'll do that, Mrs. Crabling. Could I see that piece of paper?"

He waited while she looked through her bag. When she showed it to him he recognised it at once. It was the index number of Hickmansworths' station wagon that had so mysteriously increased its mileage by forty during the night of Saturday to Sunday.

Chapter Eighteen

Snow came into the Duke of Clarence, leaving his 'team' in two cars.

"Congratulations, Mr. Deene," he said, with a cordiality that seemed to Carolus a trifle forced. "There must be a lot you know that you haven't told me. Or was it luck?"

"It was luck. I told you it was a long shot, but it came up. All I knew was that Hickmansworth grew up here and the Neasts used to stay with him as boys. We owe it to the landlord of this pub that he remembered the whereabout of their secret headquarters when Hickmansworth led the gang more than thirty years ago."

"Anyway, you've found it. We'll get to work on it right away. Are you coming? Or will the landlord show us the place?"

"I'm not coming. I'm tired and sickened by this thing and I've got to start teaching tomorrow."

"Look here, Mr. Deene. You can't just walk out like that, knowing more than you've told me."

"If you would like to come and dine with me on Saturday, I will promise to tell you everything I've gathered about all this. But it won't be much more than guesswork with a few bits of circumstantial evidence to back it."

"I wish you'd tell me this evening. The next two days are critical."

"I simply can't. I've worked like a beaver on this case and I want some rest from it. It's pretty nauseating. But on Saturday . . ."

"All right. I'll accept that."

"Meanwhile I have something to ask you, or advise you if you like, with all the urgency I can command."

"What's that?" asked Snow rather indifferently. "I must get to the body."

"Look, Snow. You don't want another murder tonight, do you? Then do what I tell you. *Arrest Cyril Neast.*"

"On what charge?"

"I don't give a damn what charge. Provided you get him under lock and key. This is not sensational nonsense, Snow. I mean exactly what I say."

"But you're totally unreal, man. Arrest a man on *any* charge? You must be out of your mind. I should lose my job tomorrow, and perhaps face charges myself. We can't just go about arresting people for your convenience."

"It's not for my sake, but yours. If you don't do it after this warning, I tell you you may be responsible for yet another death."

"But I must charge him with something."

"Charge him with the murder of Humby. Or of Grossiter. Or Darkin. It really doesn't matter, so long as you put him away tonight."

"On what evidence?"

"His fingerprints on Hickmansworths' car will do, surely?"

"Mr. Deene, I don't know what would happen to you if you were in the CID. You wouldn't last long, I'm afraid."

"Oh, to hell with the CID," said Carolus. "One life at least is at stake here. Have that man arrested before nightfall or you'll regret it for the rest of your life."

"While you quietly drive off home?"

"I can't do any more. I've no powers of arrest. You can work out the formalities, Snow. It can't be as difficult as that. Arrests have been made on lesser grounds."

"All right. I'll do it. But you realise that it will bring every newspaper out with headlines. If I can't find the proof afterwards . . ."

"There'll be plenty of proof. I promise you that."

"I thought you said you had only guesswork to offer," said Snow rather bitterly, turning away.

"There will be plenty of proof if you make that arrest."

On that they parted, Snow to go out with his team to the Dane-hole, Carolus to drive back to Newminster. But Carolus was satisfied that he had achieved what he intended—Cyril Neast would be arrested.

Carolus decided to return to Newminster via Hallows End and pick up the bag he had left at the Falstaff, for he hoped that he would not have to visit that grim village again. He waited only to thank the landlord of the Duke of Clarence for his vitally important help, then drove off. He felt dispirited and dull. He knew the truth about this unpleasant case, but he was not as sure as he had pretended to be that there would be a conviction.

It was an hour after leaving Snow that he entered the Falstaff and found Mr. Sporter full of news.

"I hear the police have found Humby's body in a house called Dane Hall at Haysdown. They've just arrested Cyril Neast. Detection-wise they don't let much grass grow under their feet."

"Are you sure Cyril Neast has been arrested?"

"Absolutely cert. Saw the Black Maria go by. He's at the police station over at Cashford by now."

"You're very well and very promptly informed."

"News-wise I like to keep abreast," said Sporter modestly. "The funny thing was the two brothers were in here at lunch-

time today. They don't often come in; I don't believe I've seen
the tall one here more than twice before. Almost teetote, I understand. I watched them pretty carefully today. I wasn't a bit
surprised to hear it was Cyril Neast they've picked up. Nasty
bit of work."

"Think so?"

"Drink-wise, I mean. He was one of those types who always pretend they're drunker than they are. Tell stories about
having 'had a few' when they did this or that. Try to make you
think they're dipso when all they drink is two or three pints at a
time. Pretty boring, I find that, conversation-wise."

"I agree."

"Cyril was a bully, too. The taller brother did most of the
talking but I thought today—he's scared stiff of Cyril."

"Have you always thought that?"

"I don't know that I've ever watched them together before.
I've always thought Cyril was a bully, though. Stonegate was
scared of him. Old Rudd was the only one who took no notice
of him. Well, I suppose he'll get life imprisonment for this. Cyril,
I mean. That's what they give them nowadays, isn't it? Even if
he has bumped off more than one."

"It was unusual for them to come in today, then? Did they
ask any questions?"

"Asked where you were. I said I'd heard you say you were
going over to Haysdown. They didn't say any more."

"Do you ever get any of the Hickmansworths in here?"

Carolus saw it coming.

"No. Hickmansworth-wise we get nothing at all. They don't
mix locally. Bit misan, all of them."

Carolus bade Sporter goodbye with the secret hope that they
would not meet again, and started driving back to Newminster,
also, he decided, for the last time.

The reception he received from Mrs. Stick was not a warm one.

"You've done it this time, sir," she said and never was the "sir" used less respectfully. "You know what there was today, don't you? A meeting of the whole staff before term starts tomorrow and you was the only one missing."

"Mrs. Stick. I'm very tired, I've been through some most unpleasant experiences today and I should like a rest and a drink before hearing anything about staff meetings."

"You'll hear about them soon enough," predicted Mrs. Stick, nevertheless bringing a tray to set beside Carolus. "Wait till the Headmaster gets on to you tomorrow. He's been on the phone today. 'Mrs. Stick,' he said, 'would you kindly tell Mr. Deene that we all await his pleasure. The staff meeting was called for four o'clock and tea has already been served.' 'He's not here, sir,' I said, 'it must have slipped his memory.' '*Slipped his memory!*' he said, 'but it is the terminal staff meeting, Mrs. Stick.' Well, what could I say? I couldn't say you were hopping about after murderers, could I?"

"No, I suppose not," agreed Carolus.

"There's only Cold for you tonight because I didn't know what time you were coming. Assy Etty on glaze, with a chocolate mouse to follow."

"*Mousse*, Mrs. Stick," said Carolus absently.

"That's what I said, isn't it? Now you have your drink in peace while I go and see about it. Stick's gone to bed."

As Carolus foresaw, his first class on the following morning was interrupted by the entrance of Muggeridge, the school porter, who resented most things about the school from the Headmaster's pomposity to the junior boys' habit of coming up behind him and tipping over his eyes the silk hat that Mr. Gorringer insisted he wear.

He spoke to Carolus in a confidential whisper loud enough for most of the class to hear.

"He's all fire and slaughter this morning," he said, not thinking it necessary to use more than a pronoun for the Headmaster. "You ought to see him. Sitting up at that blasted desk of his like a heathen image. 'Present Mr. Deene with the Headmaster's compliments,' he says, 'and tell him I should be glad if he will step over here in the Break.' I felt like asking him why he didn't ask you himself when he saw you in chapel, but what's the good? He wants all the trimmings, so he better have them, I suppose. Anyway I've told you, haven't I?"

Carolus decided on a breezy approach and, on entering Mr. Gorringer's study and finding him sitting erect behind his desk, he did not give him a chance to speak first.

"I was coming over in any case, Headmaster," he said, "to ask you if you happen to be free for dinner tomorrow."

Mr. Gorringer raised his hand.

"I'm sorry to say, Mr. Deene, that before we can go into these lighter matters, there is a *mauvais quart d'heure* before us. I was astounded yesterday to find you neglecting the elementary courtesy of attending the small tea party which I gave the staff on the afternoon before we reassemble."

"I know. It was disgraceful of me. But I had to get that Hallows End case settled before term began."

Mr, Gorringer sternly cleared his throat.

"Am I to understand, Mr. Deene, that you were absent from a gathering that from both politeness and duty you should have attended, in order to pursue your insane hobby of so-called criminal investigation? That you neglected us in order further to embarrass an already overworked and efficient police force?"

"I found Humby's body yesterday."

"I must request your silence, Mr. Deene. I want no reference made to the details of your unfortunate hobby. We waited
for you . . . Did you say you found Humby's body?"

"What's left of it, yes."

Mr. Gorringer joined the tips of his fingers.

"While in no way countenancing your neglect of your right-
ful profession, Deene," he began, "I cannot help but admit that
I have seen in the morning's newspaper that poor Humby has
been found. Am I to understand that this was due to your researches? If so, it may put a slightly different complexion on my
displeasure."

"Not my researches. Sheer luck."

"I also observed in my casual glance at the newsprint that
an arrest had been made. Was this also in some way due to
you?"

"I persuaded Snow to charge him, yes."

"Then I suppose that once again I find the ground cut away
from under my feet. I must overlook your defection in view of
your success in a case which so nearly touches the school. But
let there be no more of it, my dear Deene. The term has now
begun and we have sterner duties to attend to."

"There's nothing more for me to do at Hallows End. It's up
to the police now."

"I am relieved to hear it. Did my ears deceive me, or did you
on first entering mention something about tomorrow evening?"

"Yes. I asked you to dinner."

"Ah. Now that we have reached this happy composition of
our differences, I shall be delighted to accept. Am I to anticipate
that some light may be thrown on events at Hallows End and at
Haysdown?"

"I've promised to give Detective Sergeant Snow my side of
the case."

"Illuminating, I feel sure. I shall anticipate it with pleasure. Meanwhile let us to our duties, Deene. Our pupils await."

That evening Carolus had a call from Snow. He had not yet got a full report on the cadaver, as he now called it, but from his own observation said it was in a terrible state.

"A first examination showed that. You've never seen anything like it. It appeared that the wretched man had been battered to death by machinery. Bones smashed and the whole surface scarred. The killer must have been mad. There can be no sane explanation of that kind of brutality."

"Terrible," said Carolus. "Do you know how long your experts think he had been dead?"

"Not yet. I shall probably know all that when I see you tomorrow. Meanwhile I'm pretty worried about Cyril."

"Why? Won't he talk?"

"Not a word, even of denial. I begin to think you've let me in for a crash over this, Mr. Deene. Super Moore says I was wise to take your advice, but what am I going to look like if I can't get more of a case together than we've got now?"

"Don't worry. You will. Doesn't Cyril say *anything*?"

"Beyond a demand to see a solicitor, nothing."

"*Which* solicitor?"

"Not his brother's, but the man Darkin intended to see, John Stuffart."

"That's good," said Carolus. "That's very good. I don't think you've anything to worry about."

"I wish I could agree. To my simple mind, it looks as though I've charged a man with murder on evidence insufficient to convict a ten-sentence recidivist with shoplifting."

"I'll see you tomorrow," promised Carolus and put the receiver down. He then rang up Humphrey Spaull and asked him and Zelia Harris to dinner on the following evening. Spaull seemed a little confused and said he would ask Zelia if she was free. He returned to the telephone, however, after a few moments in calmer mind, and said they would be delighted to accept. But Carolus did not invite Thripp and Molly Caplan, nor did he communicate with Theodora Humby.

"Six for dinner tomorrow," he told Mrs. Stick. "Mr. and Mrs. Gorringer, Mr. Spaull and Miss Harris, Mr. Snow and I."

"Well, it will be a nice change, sir, I'm sure for you to entertain a little after all this running about. I see they've caught this fellow down at Hallows End, so you won't have that on your mind. Mistr'an Mrs. Gorringer always find something nice to say about the dinner. Mr. Spaull and his young lady are those that came with his head bound up that Sunday morning, aren't they? But may I be so bold as to ask who 'Mr.' Snow might be?"

"Detective Sergeant Snow, Mrs. Stick. In charge of the Hallows End case. You know him perfectly well."

"Well, you know what you're doing, I've no doubt, only I can't see that Mistr'an Mrs. Gorringer will want to mix with policemen and such. I know I shouldn't if I was them."

"What will you give us, Mrs. Stick?"

"I thought you might start with a nice game soup, soup der chess as they say."

"*Soupe de Chasse*," translated Carolus. "Yes?"

"Then a nomlet nice was . . ."

"*Omelette Niçoise*. Certainly."

"Then how about a blanket der vow?"

"*Blanquette de Veau*. Excellent."

"With creeps to finish up with."

"*Crêpes*, yes. Only not that overrated Suzette business."

"Certainly not, sir. I wasn't thinking of it. Creeps hoax noicks was what I had in mind."

"*Aux noix*," said Carolus who was proficient in Mrs. Stick's terminology. "Yes, that will be better."

"You pound walnuts with pistachios and warm cream," explained Mrs. Stick.

"Eight o'clock then," said Carolus.

CHAPTER NINETEEN

DINNER WAS FINISHED, Mr. Gorringer had pronounced it Lucullan, "positively Lucullan, my dear Deene," Mrs. Gorringer had made a *mot* about a skeleton at the feast, at which her husband had laughed, Spaull had looked shy and Zelia more spirited than usual, while Snow had observed with some wonderment his fellow guests.

It was time for Mr. Gorringer to assume the role, so dear to him, of a chairman presenting a guest speaker.

"And now my dear Deene," he exhorted, "let us to a more intellectual treat. We await your elucidation of events at Hallows End with an eagerness it goes hard to conceal. Will you not expound?"

Carolus, accustomed to Mr. Gorringer's flamboyance, heard the exordium unmoved, but, having lit a cigar, began quietly.

"An interesting case because the puzzle did not primarily lie in detecting a murderer but rather in establishing whether there had been a murder. In other words, this was not so much a who-done-it as a who-done-what."

"Excellent," said Mr. Gorringer.

"At least, I cannot think that anyone could seriously doubt from the first that Holroyd Neast was the man. You could not have two such obviously homicidal lunatics in one group of people, certainly not two with such motives, opportunity and ruthlessness as Holroyd had. The only way in which anyone else could be suspected was by going on that outworn principle of choosing the *least* likely person and gambling on him or her. By that method you might, I suppose, have had suspicions of Hickmansworth, Spaull, Thripp or even Mrs. Caplan or the Rector, but it would have been an artificial case not founded on logic or deduction. It could only be Holroyd aided by Cyril or Darkin, or both, and Holroyd was undoubtedly guilty.

"But guilty of what? That is what perplexed me all through and I cannot even now answer the question with any certain proof. I have little more than a hypothesis to offer. It convinces me, but it certainly would not convince a court of law unless it were confirmed, as I believe it will be, by a rush of incontrovertible evidence. Of that I will talk later.

"If one could accept the enormous coincidence that Grossiter had died naturally at such a supremely convenient moment as just before signing a new will which would dispossess his relations and manservant, it was plain sailing. Grossiter had died and Humby had been got rid of, either before reaching him or after Grossiter had signed. But I can never accept coincidence and had to search elsewhere for an explanation of events.

"I am frequently criticised for spending too much time in listening to the often irrelevant statements of witnesses and encouraging them to talk. So I must in self-defence point out that it was from two just such seeming irrelevancies that I obtained the key to this whole problem. Mrs. Humby said of her husband's physical culture, 'He was not fit, really. A dickie heart ever since he had rheumatic fever. Dr. Boyce told him so a dozen times.' This I was able to confirm with Dr. Boyce. Humby's heart was in a very bad condition and might fail him at any minute.

"The other remark came from Holroyd Neast. I asked him if Monk's Farm belonged to him. 'To me and my brother,' he said. 'We bought it for a song. If there's one thing I pride myself on, it's being able to seize an opportunity when I see one. I think it's one of the most important things in life.' Put those two statements from different people together and the whole problem becomes clear. Duncan Humby, after a particularly heavy lunch with his partner, and a fast drive of sixty miles, had a heart attack and died quite naturally in his car in Church Lane, Hallows End, and Holroyd Neast, seeing his opportunity, took advantage of it.

"Let us put ourselves in the position of the Neast brothers as they drove home that Monday afternoon. After many years in which they had not the slightest hope of anything from Grossiter's estate, the doors of promise had opened an inch or two. Their uncle had announced his intention of coming to stay with them with the object, they must have guessed, of considering them as his heirs. But his stay had been a failure. Poverty or parsimony had prevented them from making him comfortable and he had disliked their characters on sight. By his treatment of young Spaull in front of them, he showed pretty plainly that neither they, nor Darkin, need expect anything from his estate if he were to make a will.

"I do not think Cyril Neast heard his uncle's telephone conversation with Humby on the Sunday morning. I think Grossiter may have told the Neasts to expect nothing from him, but not that his solicitor was due on Monday to implement this. I think they may have discussed the possibility of murdering him, and were fairly sure that Darkin, for a share of the spoils, would join them. The Neasts regarded the making of any will by Grossiter as assuring their own disinheritance, for they believed Grossiter to be intestate and that they were his only heirs. None of them knew of the previous will: the old man had always sworn he would die intestate so that his son would inherit, and he had given Humby such injunctions about the secrecy of that will that Humby had not even told his partner, and kept the will in his private safe.

"If they had known that Humby was coming that day, I don't think they would have calmly gone to market. I think they would have planned some clumsy way to prevent the will being signed. But I may be wrong about this. It is one of those questions that can only be answered by the Neasts themselves. It's not very important, perhaps, but it's annoying to find no strong evidence to support one view or the other. It will not materially affect events if we assume that Grossiter's telephone call to Humby on that Sunday morning was not overheard and that as the Neasts drove home from market they had no knowledge of the solicitor's promised visit.

"Then Holroyd was given, and seized, his opportunity. As they drove up Church Lane towards their home at about five o'clock that Monday afternoon, they found a car blocking their way. They got out and found Humby dead at the wheel. Holroyd's knowledge of medicine enabled him to diagnose the cause of death—a heart attack. What could be more convenient? What could be handier than the corpse of a man of their uncle's age, a man *who had died naturally*? Dr. Jayboard had never set eyes on their uncle. All they had to do was to call Jayboard to examine this corpse as that of their uncle and they would have an impeccable death certificate with which to cremate Grossiter when they had murdered him. They put Humby's body in the back of their lorry, drove or pushed his car to the side of the road in order to pass, and drove on the farm.

"Our only outside information of what happened that evening comes from Humphrey Spaull. He saw that Holroyd was driving the lorry and stopped outside the Neasts' bungalow only long enough to get out and hand the wheel to Cyril. Cyril then locked the lorry away in a barn among the farm buildings, the body of Humby remaining in it till after dark, presumably.

"I find it interesting to speculate about what went on in that dreadful little bungalow between those three most unattractive men. It cannot be more than speculation at present, though, as I say, I think we shall have very complete information in time. Let us suppose that the brothers took Darkin into their confidence, and that Darkin, who had realised from what Grossiter said to Spaull that he would get nothing for his seventeen years of faithful service from Grossiter's estate, agreed to join the conspiracy, the Neasts promising a certain proportion of the money when they inherited it, as no one doubted they would. Incidentally, a small question arises here to which we may never know the answer. What had happened between Grossiter and Darkin since the making of that other will by which Darkin benefitted so disproportionately? Perhaps Mrs. Cupper may be able to tell anyone curious enough to enquire.

"Till now, according to our supposition, they did not know who Humby was. He was just a dead man of Grossiter's age. Plenty of people, Puckett told me, drove up Church Lane to see that particularly fine church and the Neasts supposed this was a chance visitor. At what point did they become aware that it was Grossiter's solicitor and that he was actually carrying the will? Darkin knew Humby by sight, so if he went over to the lorry he could have told the others what they had to deal with. It must have been a considerable shock to them. A man, any man, disappearing from near their house might not draw attention to them unduly. That was a risk Holroyd had calculated and was prepared to take. But the disappearance of their uncle's solicitor, as he brought a will to their uncle that disinherited them, would certainly raise a hue and cry and involve them hopelessly in suspicion. For this reason, I think it was not until after Grossiter had been murdered that Darkin discovered and revealed Humby's identity, and then it was too late to turn back. The wonderful opportunity seen by Holroyd had turned into a very risky business indeed, from which there was no retreat.

"They might, of course, have driven Humby's car to some place as far as possible from their home. But they probably calculated that Stonegate must have seen it, and the man in it, on his way home, and thought that others, the Rector perhaps or Mrs. Rudd, may have noticed it. Besides, if one of them was seen driving it or leaving it, or driving away from it in their lorry, it would involve them more absolutely than the finding of it in Church Lane would do. They preferred—wisely perhaps—to face what could only be suspicion rather than risk some unanswerable proof of their involvement. Their whole attitude argues this. When I interviewed them, I realised that all three knew they were under the gravest suspicion and had prepared their answers to almost every possible question.

"How was Grossiter murdered? This again we shall know in time, but for the moment let us assume that it was through Holroyd's knowledge of medicine that he could be killed without scars or distorted features, or any of the results of violence. He was probably poisoned.

"They brought Humby's body over from the farm building in the lorry to avoid carrying it through the lane, probably. We know this because Spaull was wakened by the lorry's lights as it was returned to its place.

"Then came the tricky business of putting Humby's body into Grossiter's bed and pyjamas and giving it the peaceful look of one who had died in his sleep. It took some nerve to wait till five-thirty in the morning before calling Dr. Jayboard, but this was necessary because of *time*. Humby had died somewhere about four p.m. or a little earlier, and Jayboard was told that the man he examined had died during the night, at the earliest ten p.m. But they calculated correctly that by letting sufficient time pass before Jayboard's examination, they could blur the issue of the exact time of death.

"Where did they put the body of Grossiter while the body of Humby was being examined? This involves some macabre possibilities. Perhaps the neighbouring bedroom was cleared and the two corpses lay in beds in two adjoining rooms. At all events, Jayboard examined Humby's body, believing it to be Grossiter's, and gave his certificate with no doubt in his mind. If you think Jayboard was careless in this, ask yourselves what doctor, called to the bedside of his neighbours' uncle whom he knows to be an elderly man staying with them, would for a moment suppose that the corpse he examined was not the right one. If someone rang you at five o'clock in the morning and said he thought his uncle was dead and would you as a doctor come and see, and if the caller, a respectable inhabitant of your village, took you into a room and showed you the body of an old gentleman who had died naturally of a heart attack, would you at once ask if this *was* the body of his uncle? Of course you wouldn't, and Holroyd knew this. That part of his plan worked splendidly.

"But they were kept busy by those two corpses. They guessed that Spaull might want to see that of Grossiter, whom he knew, and that Grossiter's must be prepared by the undertaker. So Grossiter's body occupied the room in which Grossiter had slept. But they must have been rather baffled when Dr. Jayboard called again later on Tuesday to make a further examination. He told me, 'Holroyd Neast was just sitting down to his tea and asked me to join him . . . A few minutes later his brother and the man Darkin came in and . . . joined us at table.' That is, after they had had time to switch back the corpses.

"It was Grossiter's body that was cremated, the body that would have been found to contain traces of poison if it had been examined, not the body of the man who had died naturally. And with its cremation was destroyed the only absolute and final proof of the guilt of Holroyd and the other two. But there remained Humby's body which had so admirably served its turn but must now be got rid of.

"It may be that Holroyd had provided for this from the first, for he was quite capable of such detailed planning. The idea was another of his uses of opportunity. Rudd had recently been buried in the churchyard and his freshly dug grave could be dug again to make room for another body above his coffin. This would leave no traces of excavation that might show anywhere else.

"Perhaps Holroyd guessed that the police would search his house and farm. He lost no time in putting his plan into execution. On the night of Wednesday, that is two days before Grossiter's cremation, two of them, or perhaps all three, dug down as far as Rudd's coffin, then threw the body of Humby in and replaced the soil. They were just finishing when Mrs. Rudd, guided by her 'instink', looked out and saw their lantern. 'They must have heard me opening the window because I could hear them shovelling back the earth as fast as they could,' she told me. She shouted at them and 'saw the light moving away in a hurry.' So much in a hurry that they did not replace the flowers properly and sent Darkin across in the morning to arrange them, as Mrs. Rudd also saw and reported.

"The three men were now sitting pretty. They had disposed of both bodies; the one containing proof against them was destroyed finally, the other as they thought buried quite securely. They could afford to answer everybody's questions most obligingly and to receive me with the most complete explanations of everything.

"But I'm always impressed by anything out of character and when I heard that the mean and avaricious Holroyd Neast was paying for a heavy slab gravestone to cover Rudd's grave, it aroused my curiosity. I decided to show this to Holroyd. Immediately after speaking of his generosity in providing a monument for Rudd, I asked him if he was superstitious. This was quite enough for Holroyd. He jumped to the conclusion that I knew the secret of Rudd's grave and decided on instant action to recover the corpse and conceal it elsewhere.

"Of that action we have no direct evidence because Spaull here was skilfully bludgeoned from behind when he was going to investigate. This time they worked in darkness while one of them remained on guard, for they had had their warning on Wednesday when Mrs. Rudd saw their light. It was decided that it would be too risky for the Neasts to use their own car for this and Cyril was sent on foot to bring Hickmansworths', for they knew from their previous acquaintance with this family about their habit of leaving their car down at the farm, a good distance from the house. Puckett saw Cyril Neast 'hurrying up the lane on foot' that Saturday evening and thought he was merely going to get drunk. He heard him return in the car that he knew was not the Neasts' and, an hour after that, drive away again, having loaded Humby's body, presumably.

"When I heard of that second scene in the churchyard, I did not know what Mrs. Rudd had seen three nights earlier. I thought Spaull had been on his way to interrupt not a disinterment but a burial. I immediately persuaded Snow to get an exhumation order, decided to watch the churchyard myself until the exhumation was made. But during the night, Mrs. Rudd told me of Wednesday night and I realised that poor Humby's body had been buried then and had now been taken away and was lost to us again.

"It was, as far as I knew for certain then, the body of a murdered man, and I saw only one hope of nailing the murderer . . ."

"And here," said Mr, Gorringer, acting his traditional part, "let us pause a moment and give Deene a chance to refresh himself. This must be an exhausting exposition."

Carolus's listeners broke into conversation, but he did not join them. He looked tired and ill. He had never worked with more intensity on a case or been so heartily disgusted with the story he unearthed. So while Mr. Gorringer bumbled portentously and Mrs. Gorringer looked for a chance to insert a witticism, Carolus silently looked over his notes.

"I'm afraid," he said when he was ready to go on, "that I am giving you a somewhat lifeless account of this crime. The truth is, it has rather got me down. I have been working against time, chiefly in order to save the life of our only remaining witness, but also to get the thing cleared before it was time to open shop. I mean the beginning of term."

"Ah, Deene," said Mr. Gorringer, "who would not forgive your facetiousness at such a time, even though it might be thought to reflect on the school? But proceed, my dear fellow, we are all agog."

"If not a-magog," added his wife.

"There was only one chance of obtaining a conviction. The three men could scarcely all be involved in the same degree, and I hoped to frighten one of them into giving Queen's Evidence. I picked on Darkin as being the likeliest and either put the idea into his head or cultivated an idea he already had. I told him of the will which Thripp had discovered by which he would benefit so lavishly and this helped to convince him that if he was to enjoy that money he must act at once. But my interview with Darkin in the so-called Snuggery of the Falstaff had aroused the Neasts' suspicions—they had followed him up to the pub and thereafter must have watched him closely, for this time a telephone conversation *was* overheard. When Darkin phoned Stuffart to make an appointment for next day, his first step to giving Queen's Evidence, one of the Neasts overheard every word and this was Darkin's death warrant.

"He was probably killed by Thelodocticylin, the poison already used for Grossiter. Then, with the remains of a tube of Somnifax, containing Thelodocticylin, in his pocket, taken out to the meadow adjoining Hickmansworths' land, where the simplest and most convincing kind of suicide was imitated with the gun that, Holroyd states, Darkin had often borrowed from him. This one, at least, would never give Queen's Evidence.

"My finding of Humby's body was lucky, but it wasn't all luck. Hickmansworth's car had done about forty miles—that gave me a radius of less than twenty from Hallows End in which to search. Hickmansworth's telling me that he had been brought up at Haysdown and that the Neasts had stayed with him there suggested that Holroyd or Cyril might have chosen familiar ground, and I thought it worth at least a try. The landlord of the Duke of Clarence with his Dane-hole was certainly lucky, but when I found him I was only following my invariable practice of starting all enquiries in the local pub.

"The state of the body seemed at first to indicate a brutal murder, but it was consistent with that body having been flung in an open grave, then buried for three days under a few tons of soil.

"I calculated that the Neasts would know by that evening that the body had been found and that even the dull-witted Cyril would see that his only chance lay in doing what Darkin had intended to do—giving Queen's Evidence. It was probably Holroyd who had actually administered the poison in the cases of both Grossiter and Darkin, so that Cyril believed his offer of Queen's Evidence would be accepted. At all events, I saw the extreme danger of Cyril being eliminated by Holroyd before he could give it, and I believed that with his death would disappear our only chance of convicting Holroyd. That is why I persuaded Snow to arrest him that night on any charge. I have no doubt that he will get his solicitor to offer Queen's Evidence and that it will be accepted. If it is not, Holroyd will go free with a few hundred thousand pounds to enjoy."

"It's all very interesting, Mr. Deene," said Snow, "but it leaves a number of questions unanswered."

"But if I know our Deene," broke in Mr. Gorringer, "that will not be for long. He will dispose of our minutest doubts. I myself have a query to put to him. You say that you distrust coincidence, Deene. Was it not, though, a remarkable coincidence that the two men, Grossiter and Humby, were both suffering from some cardiac affliction?"

"I don't think so. Most men of sixty-five have heart trouble of some kind, after all. I imagine that Grossiter's was more obvious and more cared-for while Humby's was more serious but deliberately ignored."

"I should like to know at what point you decided that Humby's body had been used to obtain a death certificate for Grossiter?" Snow asked.

"At no point. I suppose it cannot be called certain even now, though when Cyril gives Queen's Evidence against his brother it will be, I think. I have told you what suggested it to me and I worked on that hypothesis throughout."

"What weight did you give to the man Stonegate's evidence?"

"Stonegate was either an ass and something of a buffoon, or else an extremely clever man who was in the Neast conspiracy. It was simply a matter of deciding which. If he was the first, his evidence was in the main to be trusted. If the second, it was doctored by Holroyd. I had no difficulty deciding that Stonegate was silly enough to be trusted. Spaull passed by Stonegate after coming into Church Lane from the footpath. That he was in fact the 'man walking away' about whom Stonegate was so annoyingly noncommital was neatly confirmed by Spaull's own statement."

Zelia said: "There's something Humphrey wants to know. Why had Grossiter been shaved when he saw his dead body?"

"Humby was clean-shaven. I suppose Holroyd, trying to think of everything, feared that Jayboard might compare notes with the undertaker or someone. I can see no other reason for it.

"One of the clumsier things those three did," Carolus went on, "would seem to be using Hickmansworths' station wagon to carry the corpse to Haysdown. And yet I don't know. How were they to know that the Hickmansworths kept an exact record of its mileage? Cyril was probably warned by his brother to leave no fingerprints, and only took his gloves off when he had to tinker with the engine. In closing the bonnet afterwards, before putting on his gloves, he made one of those small but all-important blunders that are so valuable to the investigator. And using that car was not their only attempt to throw suspicion on Hickmansworth. Darkin's body was carefully placed near the boundary at the point where a track had once run from one farm to the other. And Holroyd's deliberate avoidance of reference to Hickmansworth in his long conversation with me was a clever double-bluff, for Holroyd's method was to be very open about things that he knew were already known."

"A clever villain," said Mr. Gorringer, wisely shaking his head.

"Madly clever," said Carolus.

"But let us end this occasion on a happier note," the Headmaster went on relentlessly. "I have my mite to contribute to the vast amount of information Deene has gathered, for I can tell you what took Lionel Thripp and Mrs. Caplan to Hallows End at a time and in a way which must have aroused suspicion. It was no less than their wish that Thripp's old friend Mr. Whiskins should consecrate their marriage. Before the end of the year they will be man and wife."

"So help them God!" said Mrs. Gorringer, confused between a *mot* and a benediction. It was the last word on Hallows End.

Keep this card in the book pocket
Book is due on the latest date stamped